CHRISTMAS BEACH PROPOSAL

CHRISTMAS BEACH

BOOK TWO

LORI WILDE

CASSIDY GRACE

ONE

Maddie Craig hated being a statistic, a cautionary tale, and a Christmas one at that.

Every year since she lived in Christmas Beach, Louisiana, Maddie would unpack the decorations and take a trip down memory lane.

It was her favorite trip of the season. Of the year, really. A lifetime of mementos carefully stored in Bubble Wrap and cotton batting. She had a collection of snow globes with snowmen, elves, trees, gifts, reindeer, or Santa Claus figurines, all on wooden bases to protect them.

She'd lined them up on the mantel.

She'd been just as careful with the pieces belonging to the Christmas village she'd been building for years. She thought it might have more shops than Christmas Beach itself. There was a bakery, a flower shop, a yarn shop, a bookstore, a firehouse, a police station, a church with a magnificent steeple, and a train depot with a track that circled the whole.

That went on the coffee table.

She'd been the most careful of all with every single decoration Alex had made in school. He made some art in elementary school and took a few classes in middle school, including painting a ceramic coaster with a fat Santa on it and sculpting a Santa hat paperweight out of clay.

She placed both items on the table next to her chair. Then she scrolled through her phone to read news, text friends, and listen to books or watch TV. More artworks made by Alex included reindeer heads from clothespins, felt stars, bells, balls, and gingerbread men decorated with glitter and hung on the tree with ribbon loops.

She'd hung all of them on the tree, but only after wrapping it in dozens of strings of tiny colored lights and hooking filler ornaments deep in the branches. When every item was perfectly placed, including the Santa hat tree topper, she'd plugged in the lights.

And promptly set the house on fire.

Not the whole house, thankfully. It was an old one, built at least a hundred years ago. Because of that, she kept a fire extinguisher upstairs and down. Alex had run for the one in the kitchen while she'd dialed 9-1-1 and bolted for the other. They'd contained the blaze. The Christmas Beach Fire Department had done the rest.

The Victorian monstrosity was too big for her to live in alone. It was really too big for her and Alex, but it had seemed perfect when she and Rob had bought it. They'd had plans for a big family, kids to fill every one of the bedrooms.

A drunk driver had put an end to those dreams shortly after Alex had turned one.

Last year's Christmas fire had occurred during the middle of his senior year of high school. They'd spent his final semester before graduation in a small furnished rental downtown while their house was cleaned and repaired.

Weeks later, when the house was done, they'd bought furniture, area rugs, and artwork. The only decorations to survive were the coaster and paperweight. Those had been far enough away from the tree to need only a good scrubbing. The heat had burst the snow globes and cracked the buildings of the village, melting every car of the train. The coaster and paperweight were now tucked away in her dresser's bottom drawer.

She and Alex had been fine, comfortable, but it hadn't been the end to his school experience she'd wanted for him. He'd be leaving home. He'd be an adult; he *was* an adult. He'd told her it didn't matter. The two of them were safe and nothing valuable had been lost. He'd been so supportive, so grown up about the whole thing.

She hadn't known it was possible to be as proud of him as she'd been.

As she was.

Now, after four months away, he was coming home from college for his first winter break. He was working up until the last minute and wouldn't arrive until Christmas Eve. After that, she'd have him with her for three weeks. And this year would be perfect.

Or it would be if she could find what she

wanted and get out of Christmas Beach's one and only department store. Problem was, everything she wanted was gone and nothing on any shelf in any store could replace what she'd lost.

"I should've done this on Black Friday."

The voice at her side belonged to her neighbor. Jeff Murphy lived directly across from her on Brown Bark Lane. His house was as large as hers, his lot larger. Most of her trees were in her back-yard while his took over his front. He'd lived there when she'd moved in. Hard to believe she and Rob had bought the house twenty-two years ago.

Had she really lived in the same house for twenty-two years?

After starting her nursing job at Christmas Beach Pediatrics, she learned Jeff was divorced. His wife left him and their twin daughters before the girls were even old enough to have known who she was.

After Rob's death, Maddie and Jeff had become close friends, single parents, near to the same age, both homebodies. That was one of the things she appreciated about him, and selfishly so. He was always around when she needed things done that she couldn't handle herself. And once they were old enough, one or the other of his daughters, both so well-adjusted, had always been up for it when she'd needed a sitter for Alex.

Two decades of win-win... at least on her side of the street.

"Why?" she asked, getting back to his Black Friday comment.

Then she glanced over, her skin warm, suddenly aware how often she'd taken advantage of his generosity, his good nature, his willing hand.

Ugh.

His face was scruffy, his whiskers as white as they were brown. It was Saturday, so he was off work, a perk of his rank and seniority. Like her, he wore jeans, a graphic T-shirt—his sporting LSU's Mike the Tiger, hers reading: Caffeine, PO, Q4H, PRN—and a lightweight hoodie. And while she wore sneakers, he wore oil-stained work boots.

He nodded at the shelves. "Better selection."

He wasn't wrong. And he really did scruffy well. She took a deep breath, searching for solid footing, unsure why she felt so off-kilter. This was Jeff. Stable, reliable, dependable, practical Jeff. "This is better than it will be two weeks from now."

"Yeah, but it would've been even better on Black Friday."

His broken record response had her smiling. "When you would've had a better chance of being trampled to death. Flat on the floor. Like a bookmark."

He reached up to scratch his scruff. "True."

She ignored the sound, the ripple of appreciation like water on her skin, and looked at the loot in his cart. "Are you decorating for Christmas Beach's entire population?"

He snorted. "Just want the house to look good for the kids."

His kids? Their kids? "Audrey and Ashley?"

"Yep. Their men. The grands. *All* the grands." He picked up a four-pack of pink glittery ornaments. Glass ornaments.

Maddie took them out of his hand and put them back. His youngest grandson was five and his oldest, if she recalled correctly, was nine. She replaced the glass ornaments with an eight-pack featuring Marvel characters and another that was Disney themed.

All of them unbreakable. "So... ten of them. And you. Wow."

"Not all of Christmas Beach wow, but yeah. Ten of them at the same time. For a week."

He was a braver man than she. "Whose idea was this?"

Slowly, he raised his hand.

She sputtered, trying not to laugh at his misery. Then she leaned close, catching a whiff of pine and woodsmoke and chilly winter air. It smelled good on him. It smelled... homey. And comfortable. And right.

"Double wow," she whispered before reluctantly moving away. "What happened to the decorations you usually use?"

"The silver and gold plastic ones with flecked-off paint?"

"That bad?" She'd seen the balls, bells, and stars on his tree along with the other ornaments that reminded her of Alex's school art. She'd just never been close enough to notice the years of wear and tear.

He looked at her then, his brown eyes clear and rested, which was rare. Then he looked at her cart. "How many trees are *you* putting up?"

Her cart was piled high with tiny white lights and tiny colored lights and icicle lights to hang outside and anywhere she could make them work. She had kept nothing electrical from last year, whether it had been used inside or out.

She was not taking a chance with worn plugs and cords.

She also had to replace her ornaments. She'd picked up quite a few after Halloween, some even before Halloween. Penny's Department Store only carried the basics: red balls, green balls, silver balls, and gold balls in assorted sizes. Some frosted glass, some smooth. Some crusted with fake snow. She frowned down at her cart.

Jeff had a point. She'd probably end up returning a lot of what she'd bought already. She didn't know why she was adding to that headache other than wanting to be sure every branch on her tree held multiple ornaments.

She was obsessive about that.

She set a box of two dozen plastic candy canes back on the shelf. "I started to go up in the attic this morning, then remembered last year."

They were silent for a while and she wondered if he remembered the smells of fires, the burnt plastic, wood, and wires.

Maddie picked up a plastic cylinder filled with tiny red-and-white-striped bells and put it back too. What was she doing here? She didn't want any of these things.

She wanted what she'd lost. What she could never get back.

Starting over was way too much work. Way too depressing.

Jeff added both items to his cart without looking at them. "I'm already tired."

She laughed, happy to have a reason to do so. "I think the word you're looking for is old."

"Speak for yourself."

"I am."

He huffed noncommittally. "Do you realize we're middle-aged? Considering life expectancy being what it is."

She'd never thought about it like that. Now she'd never be able to stop doing the math. Great. "We're probably past middle age."

They stood still for a moment while shoppers grabbed Christmas decorations around them. Neither one of them moved, as if on a mission and refusing to give up, too set in their ways, too old.

Ugh.

"Bet you can't wait to see Alex," Jeff said, bringing Maddie back from death's door.

"I'm counting the days. The hours. I haven't yet made it to the minutes."

"But?"

She waved her hand in front of the display. "It's not the same."

And that was the crux of her balance issues, wobbling between joyful and morose. As her son had told her last year, nothing had been lost that couldn't be replaced, and the two of them had come away unscathed. But he'd been eighteen. He hadn't just lost a lifetime of physical reminders of his childhood holidays the way she had.

She could still remember the memories vividly, but holding the clothespin reindeer head reminded her of the gap-toothed smile Alex gave her when she hung it up for him that year.

"Because it's all new?" Jeff asked, shifting to the side to meet her gaze. He lifted a knowing brow. "And fireproof?"

"Ha-ha. But yeah. None of this will mean anything."

"It will if you make it so."

She cocked her head. "Thanks, Picard."

He blinked with confusion, then he grinned, then he let out a snorting laugh. "Nice."

He was so easy to talk to, to joke with, to be herself with, and she was tired of talking about her life. "It's new for you, too. If you think about it."

He frowned. "How so?"

"When was the last time you entertained all ten of your kids and grands?"

"Never."

"Exactly."

"So here we are."

"Yep."

"Lost in the aisles of the five-and-dime."

She huffed. "Nothing in Penny's has ever cost five. Or a dime."

"I miss the good old days."

"When there were no frozen pizzas?"

He narrowed his gaze at her. "Have you been looking in my freezer?"

"Just your recycle bin."

"Speaking of groceries..."

"Were we?"

He gave her a side-eye. "I'm going to need to fill the larder."

To say the least. "I love grocery shopping. It's like... therapy."

His laugh was skeptical. "For ten kids and grands?"

Hmm. "When do they get here?"

"Ashley and her bunch arrive late Christmas Eve. Audrey and hers early Christmas morning. They all leave on the first."

Did he have a clue what he was in for? "And you volunteered for this?"

He sighed and scrubbed a hand down his face, resigned, weary. Or at least putting on a good show. His eyes were sparkling. She bet he couldn't wait.

"Ashley mentioned her in-laws would not be home for Christmas. Then Audrey mentioned her in-laws wouldn't be home for Christmas. I couldn't decide whether they were ganging up on me or angling for an invitation."

Sounded like both. Maddie chuckled to herself. "You went with the invite."

"They caught me at a weak moment."

"More like you jumped at the chance," she said, and he bobbed his head, though she wasn't sure if he was agreeing or thinking.

Turned out to be the latter.

"You know," he said, looking from her cart to his to the shelves again, then at her. "The Christmas Market is open this weekend. I bet they have more Santarific items to choose from."

"Santarific?"

"I've noticed your decorating theme once or twice. Before last year."

When it had gone up in smoke. "All those poor Santas."

"I'm sure you miss them."

She nodded. "Not as much as I miss all the things Alex made in school, but yes."

"Well?"

She had a date next Saturday to shop the market's sale day with a friend from work. But she could do both, right? This weekend and next? Because Jeff wasn't wrong.

She missed her Santas fiercely.

Two

Christmas

Beach

The Christmas Beach Christmas Market was a madhouse of the very best sort. The air in the civic center smelled like pine, like cinnamon and cloves simmering in cider, like coffee and hot chocolate and peppermint.

Maddie stood just inside the doors and closed her eyes as she breathed it all in, her skin tingling with an incredible happiness.

It was the excitement of the holiday season.

It was Alex coming home in three weeks.

That was all. Nothing more.

It was not about Jeff. It was not about being here with Jeff.

Except it was.

Christmas music played over the sound system just loud enough to be enjoyed but not so loud that the shoppers and vendors had to shout to be heard. And there were a lot of both. Most of the vendors were local, but there were always booths —more flashy, more polished—run by those who saw Christmas as a profession, not a heartfelt pastime. Maddie always gravitated to the hobbyists.

She moved farther into the cavernous space, Jeff a few steps behind her, speaking to someone who'd hailed him on their way in. She waited, listening to the joyous cacophony, music and laughter and chatter and somewhere jingling bells.

She couldn't decide where to start. Left or right?

"Black Friday. I'm just saying."

"Uh, pretty sure this was your idea."

"Was it?"

She nudged her elbow into Jeff's arm. Curmudgeon. "Yes. It was. And a very good one," she said, waving one arm expansively. "Look at this selection."

"Look at this crowd."

She ignored him. "I smell cookies."

"I say we start there." He took hold of her elbow to keep her close, and maybe to keep her from gouging him again. And since she hadn't seen a sign, and the crowd *was* way larger and more boisterous than she'd realized, she let him.

But that was the only reason why.

His grip was firm as he made certain she wasn't mowed down by distracted shoppers and kids on a holiday high. And, she had to admit, she enjoyed having him near, not even once feeling over-whelmed by the crush of people.

Black Friday would've been so much worse. She wondered if the thought had crossed his mind. "So why *didn't* you shop on Black Friday?"

"Work. Grass fire near Piney Creek took down Joel Prejean's barn." He pointed toward several stalls against the back wall. A big sign above read, REFRESHMENTS.

"Oh. I hadn't heard. That it was Joel's, I mean." And even then, she wasn't sure she'd thought about Jeff at the scene. Jeff in danger. Jeff in harm's way.

A shiver of hot emotion worked its way to her feet.

Fighting fires was his job. It had been his job the entire time she'd known him. He did it every day. So why was she suddenly struck by the fact that he and the men he commanded put their lives on the line?

Was it because she'd finally seen him in action last year?

He maneuvered her to a stall with large chocolate chunk cookies wrapped in red cellophane and tied with green ribbons. He held up two fingers and fished his wallet from his pocket. "As fast as Christmas Beach news travels, which surprises me."

She shook off her thoughts of moments before; he wasn't wrong about that. Yet she couldn't help but wonder what had brought them on in the first place.

Why here? Why now?

"Thanks." She took the cookies he handed her. "It may have slipped in one ear and out the other. Work has been crazy busy. We've had so many kids with respiratory problems this year. Worse than usual."

"I can believe it," he said as they moved to the

next stall. "Ashley's asthma seemed to always flare up when the cold hit."

"I remember," Maddie said, digging cash from her pocket and paying for their drinks. "Do you have to work while everyone's here?"

"Thank you," he said to the vendor who handed them lidded cups of homemade hot chocolate. "And thank you," he said to Maddie, shaking his head. "I worked Thanksgiving weekend to clear Christmas. But I've also got a lot of vacation saved up."

She bet he did. Over the years, there'd only been a handful of times he'd asked her to keep an eye on his place and collect his mail while he was away. "And seniority."

"True, but most of the guys have families. I don't, at home, anyway, so I don't mind working the holidays. It's easier for me."

"You're a nice man," she said, breaking off half a cookie, then wrapping the rest and dropping the package into her purse. Jeff handed her his to carry with hers.

He sipped his cocoa and ignored her comment. "How's your schedule?"

She stopped at a table with wooden folk art ornaments. They were painted in distressed reds and greens. She picked up a set of three Santas and had the shopkeeper ring her up. "I'm free the week of Christmas, but I'll have to go back after the first. Alex's classes start up a couple of weeks after that."

"So we're off at the same time."

"Seems so," she said, trying not to read anything into his remark.

"It'll be good to see Alex. We'll have to grill steaks one night."

"He would love that." She would love that. Even if steaks for ten plus two would cost a small fortune. It was the holiday season. And overspending during the holiday season, especially on family, didn't count. Overspending on decorations, however...

They stopped in front of a booth selling playful clay ornaments. Maddie picked up a reindeer with a bulbous red nose and crossed eyes and couldn't resist. While the vendor rang up the sale, her thoughts drifted again.

She thought about all the times she and Alex had thrown chicken on the grill and had Jeff and the girls join them. Or how often Audrey or Ashley, or both, had run across the street to tell Maddie their dad wanted her and Alex to come for burgers and dogs.

Audrey had always screwed up her nose and assured Maddie the dogs weren't really dogs, just wieners, but not wiener dogs, either. The fraternal twin girls didn't care about matching clothes or keeping their hair tidy.

Jeff had done an amazing job as a single father. He'd missed one or two school events, asking Maddie to stand in for him. She had, getting the girls home, bathed, and tucked in, then waiting for Jeff, Alex beside her asleep on the couch.

Jeff had helped Alex with math and been at every football game he could manage. Maddie had tutored his girls in chemistry, one of her favorite subjects. She'd also taken them out to practice driving so Jeff wouldn't have a heart attack.

Their two families had functioned as one.

But they hadn't been.

Alex had asked her once, when he was four, why he didn't have a daddy because everyone had a daddy. She remembered it vividly, the way he'd thrown out one arm, how his voice had spilled his sad confusion.

Maddie shook off the melancholia and reached for the rest of her cookie because cookies made everything better. She breathed in the aromas of sugar and spice and sang along with the carols. It had to be waiting for Alex that had her so emotional today.

Alex being away for the first time, and all her preparations requiring new ornaments, and losing tradition and mementos and starting over.

Ugh.

But she'd be fine, she told herself, just as Jeff asked, "You okay?"

"Nothing this cookie won't fix," she said, then dug for his package and handed it to him. "Trust me. One bite and you'll forget how much money you've already spent."

"I'd like to forget how much I've still got to have to spend. Gifts. Food..."

Maddie handed him her second cookie. And then she handed him her purse as her attention was snagged by a set of candles... eight reindeer, a sleigh, and a very rotund Santa. She looked up at Jeff.

"I have to have this for my mantel."

"Go for it."

She lowered her voice. "It's a small fortune."

But he didn't talk her out of it like she'd thought he might. Maybe even hoped he might. She had no self-control with Saint Nick.

Jeff pulled the ribbon from the cookies. "Consider it your Christmas gift to yourself."

She held his gaze as he inhaled half a cookie. "Do you buy gifts for yourself?"

"All year long," he said after a swig of cocoa. "At the sporting goods store."

"You're no help," she grumbled. She paid the candlemaker. His assistant carefully secured each piece of the set in Bubble Wrap, adding more bubbles between them as she stacked them in a shopping bag.

Maddie turned back to Jeff. "This will weigh a ton."

He held out one arm, flexing. She hooked the bag's handles over his elbow. Then she took his two smaller bags and slid them onto her shoulder. "Are you going to poop out on me? We only have two aisles left."

"Is there a rule stating we have to shop all of them?"

She nodded. "Yes. An unwritten one."

He chuckled beneath his breath. "Lead the way."

Far too soon, because Maddie was enjoying Jeff's company far too much, it was time to go. Yes, it was a Saturday, but she still had a lot of items to cross off her weekend to-do list. Plus, they'd circled the perimeter of the civic center and made their way up and down both side of every aisle. She had no more shopping in her.

"Ready if you are," she said.

"Right behind you."

The building was stuffy. When they opened the front doors, they felt a blast of chilly air that promised winter. It smelled of fireplace smoke and icy cold frost.

The forecast hadn't predicted a white Christmas this year. Christmas Beach rarely saw snow or sleet, and only occasionally freezing temperatures. She kinda liked that.

No ice on the roads. No snow to shovel. No trees down because of branches weighted with frozen precipitation. No loss of power.

The kids hated it, of course. They wanted to build jumbo snowmen, not the ones they managed with snowballs the size of walnuts... if they were lucky. No sledding. No ice skating on ponds. But all of that meant fewer broken bones or lacerations from fights with icicle daggers. She snorted, crossing the parking lot beside Jeff.

She wasn't sure if she sounded like a helicopter

parent, a fuddy-duddy, or a nurse who'd seen her fair share of injuries which, she admitted, happened no matter the season. She just hated seeing the little ones sidelined when it was time for Santa.

She dug for her keys and clicked open her cargo hatch. Jeff opened his truck's back door. Her bags slid from her arms to the floor, and she groaned, stretching her arms high overhead. "I am never doing this again. Not without a cart."

Jeff laughed, slamming the back door to his truck parked next to her SUV. "Nice haul, though. Now all that's left are the trees. And the presents. And the menu."

"You want to combine forces?" She gulped, hoping she'd done so fast enough to grab back the words and swallow them. Alas, she had not.

Jeff's frown was curious. "How so?"

"I'll help you cook," she heard herself saying, the words coming out before she thought twice or thought better or even thought at all. "You help me hang lights."

"That's not exactly a fair division of labor," he said, watching as she opened her front door and tossed her purse to the passenger seat.

She wrapped her hoodie tight as a brisk breeze

swept through the rows of cars. "I didn't say I'd do all the cooking. You'd help."

His brows rose at that. "But you won't help with the lights."

"I'll tell you where they need to go. You hang them. And most importantly, you plug them in. While your fire engine idles at the curb."

"Isn't that going a bit overboard?" he asked, amusement in his tone and in his twinkling eyes.

She found nothing overboard or amusing in what she'd said. "In plugging in my Christmas lights, there is no such thing."

"Got it. You supervise. I hang, plug, and keep the engine running."

Perfect. "After church tomorrow. Come for lunch. We'll make up a calendar of meals for the week with your family. Then put together a shopping list from that." When he frowned, she added, "You did say something about your larder."

"The cupboard is definitely bare."

She wondered what he *did* have to work with. "And that deep freeze in your garage?"

"Mostly frozen pizza and ice cream."

"Is that why the weight bench is blocking access?"

"I moved it."

"I see."

"You know," he said, picking up a pine cone decorated in gold glitter stars and fake snow, turning it over and around in his hand before setting it back in the bag in the rear of her SUV. "There's no reason for both of us to cook Christmas dinner."

"Uh, yes, there is," she responded before hit with what he was saying. Because then she was hit with an apprehension she couldn't define. Her skin tingled to the chilly wind biting her.

"Uh, no, there's not," he said while she was still processing how she felt about what she was certain was coming. He pulled down her hatch, shoving hard until the lock caught and clicked. "You and Alex come eat with us. One big happy family."

That, right there, she mused, pulling in chilly air, was why she knew his idea was the best thing she'd ever heard.

And the absolute worst.

THREE

Though she'd never admitted it to anyone—she had enough trouble as it was admitting it to herself—Maddie had been in love with Jeff Murphy for more years than she wanted to acknowledge, but last year's fire had cinched the deal.

No going back. In over her head. Head over heels. Whatever.

Unable to escape the truth and forced to accept

it—along with the depth of her feelings for Jeff—hadn't been that hard. The hard part came next.

Figuring out what to do about it.

Because she couldn't go on the way she had been, ruffled and flustered and shooing away the butterflies in her midsection that reminded her of being thirteen.

She was not thirteen. It had been ages since she'd been in her teens.

When Alex's next birthday rolled around, her son would turn twenty.

She had to get a grip. To act her age, a thought that made her groan. Age was just a number, right? Thirteen or thirty—or in her case, forty-eight—made no difference to the butterflies. This wasn't about age. It was about her being in love with Jeff.

She pushed the thought to the back of her mind with all the others she kept there. Maybe they were all surfacing because the vault was full. Because she'd been pushing them to the back of her mind for so many years. Because she hadn't had time or space or energy to face them. And now her mind vault was forcing her hand.

Ugh.

Her kitchen was clean. The sink empty, the dishwasher unloaded, the top of the range scrubbed clear of every dried crumb. Same with the countertops. Same with the floor.

When was the last time she'd spic-and-spanned her kitchen for another person?

Maybe when Alex was in high school and had friends over? Nope. Maybe when Alex was in middle school and she'd hosted the end-of-year eighth-grade party-planning committee? Nope. Maybe when Alex was in elementary school, and she'd thrown him the biggest, baddest birthday party a ten-year-old had ever imagined? Nope.

And this was Jeff Murphy. *Jeff Murphy*. Her neighbor. One of the firefighters who'd seen her house in the worst state it had ever been in. Fire aside.

After rolling out of bed super early this morning, she'd put a pot roast and a pound of carrots into the slow cooker while her coffee had brewed. She'd downed her first cup in the shower. Now on her second, she tossed in the potatoes, then headed back to her room to dress. Everything would be ready to eat after church.

She'd even found two legal pads and pens and set them on the table so she and Jeff could make their holiday menu notes and a shared shopping list.

Easy peasy. A Sunday like any other.

With the man she loved.

Groaning, she stared at her reflection in her bedroom's full-length Cheval mirror. Black flats. Dressy black slacks. A nubby sweater the color of eggplant with threads of gold woven throughout. The delicate gold chain Alex had given her for *his* high school graduation. That son of hers. Four months had never seemed so long.

He could not get here soon enough. She was giddy with anticipation and counting down the days, missing every bit of his noise: his thunderous footsteps up and down the stairs, the doors he only knew how to slam. What was it with teenagers?

And on his next birthday, he'd leave his teens behind.

How in the world was she old enough to be the mother of a twenty-year-old?

We're middle-aged.

"Thanks, Jeff," she grumbled as she grabbed her purse and left the room, thinking that at least they were middle-aged together. Somehow that made it easier to accept her spring chicken days were behind her, and she was facing cronehood.

Walking across the church parking lot, she waved at the parents of several of her small patients. The little ones waved, too, a couple of them frowning and asking her, as they did every Sunday, why she wasn't wearing her clothes with the dogs eating giant bones.

"My favorite clothes are the ones with the polar bears and black bears and pandas," said eight-year-old Kimmy Lang after her five-year-old sister Cindy walked all around Maddie, looking for the dogs and the bones.

"C'mon, girls," their father, Keith, said, urging them to hurry. "You're going to be late to Sunday school."

Their mother, Jenna, walked into the building with Maddie. "You look great, by the way. That color is perfect on you."

"Even without the dog bones?" Maddie asked, and Jenna laughed.

"It's funny how we get so used to seeing someone in a certain setting that it can take a minute to place them when we run into them elsewhere."

Like seeing Jeff Murphy in Penny's? Though placing him hadn't been an issue. She'd seen him in jeans, suit pants, cargo shorts... even in his turnout gear with his face covered in soot. Over the years, she'd run into him at school events, in the bank's drive-through line, picking up to-go orders at Bakers Dozen.

He was as much a part of Christmas Beach's scenery as she was.

Great. Now she was scenery. Middle-aged scenery.

She said goodbye to Jenna and tried not to feel even older than she was.

And then it hit her.

The root of her upheaval wasn't about loving Jeff. It was about the fire and seeing him in a different emotional light—one that had picked a really inconvenient time to shine.

It was Christmas. Alex would be home soon. She had to get the house ready for him, which basically meant stocking up on all his favorite foods. She had to decorate and shop and wrap gifts. Jeff would have to wait.

Right.

Though they attended the same worship services, she and Jeff never rode or sat together. Sometimes he sat alone. Other times with a fellow firefighter's family or with one of the friends he had in Christmas Beach. And he had a lot of friends.

Maddie usually sat with one of three women

she'd met while Alex was in school and stayed close to over the years. Two were single mothers of boys he'd played football with. The third, Lisa Olsen, also a widow, had been a room mother when her daughter was in the same first-grade class as Alex.

Sliding in next to her now, Maddie asked, "Are you ready for Chelsea to get home?"

"You have no idea—" Lisa stopped and gave a soft, desperate laugh. "Sorry. Forgot who I was talking to there for a minute. Of course, you have an idea."

"Aww. It's okay." Maddie leaned closer, wrapping her arm around Lisa's shoulders for a quick hug, getting a subtle hint of her flowery perfume. "We are so in this anxiety boat together. And some days I think mine's sinking."

"Tell me about it. I'm nearly out of my mind with excitement. I didn't know four months could take so long to pass because I'm used to time flying by."

"Which is exactly what will happen, you know. Alex and Chelsea will be here for winter break, and then they'll be gone again in the snap of our fingers."

The pews were rapidly filling, the crowd's chatter growing louder. The air smelled of pine and cold, the scents rushing in each time the doors opened and closed. The auditorium was brightly lit, the morning sun blazing through the high windows on the north wall. Seasonal colors flashed in skirts and ties and glittery earrings. Maddie's own were tiny silver bells that gave off a whisper of a jingle when her hair brushed them, the sound soft and lovely and always unexpected.

"Just so you know..." Lisa screwed up her nose and let the sentence trail.

Uh-oh. Maddie gave Lisa her full attention. "What?"

"Carl Moore called me last night and mentioned seeing you and Jeff together at Penny's yesterday—"

"Where," Maddie interrupted to explain, "we ran into each other—"

"And Rose Foster messaged me not long after saying she'd seen the two of you shopping at the Christmas Market where, according to her, you looked like anything but friends and neighbors. She wanted to know if she'd missed an update."

"An update?"

"On the two of you. Your relationship."

"Oh, good grief." Christmas Beach's gossip mill was spinning at top speed.

Lisa crossed her legs, smoothing her navy skirt over her knees. The soft tint on her nails was a perfect match, but Lisa was always impeccably coordinated. The tight smile she offered Maddie was both commiserating and apologetic.

She reached for her hymnal. "I thought you might want to know."

"Thanks," Maddie said with a sigh, tucking her purse in the corner at her hip and sliding her hymnal from the pew's rack.

"But now you have to tell me everything," Lisa leaned close to say.

Maddie's heart thumped. Her nape tingled with perspiration. She'd only just made sense of what was going on. She wasn't ready to spill those beans, not even to Lisa who knew her better than almost anyone in Christmas Beach. "Tell you everything about what?"

Lisa arched a brow. "You and Jeff?"

"Me and Jeff what?"

"Are y'all together? Did you finally hook up?"

A flush spread across Maddie's chest, rising higher. She opened her hymnal and stared down. "What do you mean, finally?"

Lisa tapped her nails on her hymnal's cover. "I

mean, everyone knows that's where the two of you are headed."

Maddie forgot how to breathe. Her skin was on fire, prickles of heat like embers or sparks hopping from her ears to her neck. "Everyone who? Where?"

Lisa laughed softly as the auditorium quieted. "You know, I can't decide if you're playing dumb or if you really are."

Maddie started to roll her eyes, but she couldn't decide if Lisa was kidding. "Dumb? Really?"

"Sorry. Not dumb. Just... not paying attention."

"To gossips?" As if she had time—

"No, silly. To the way Jeff Murphy looks at you."

Gobsmacked, Maddie didn't ask Lisa what she was talking about because it was time for the opening prayer and song service. She did her best to clear her mind but found her thoughts drifting away too often.

Drifting to Jeff, looking at her in Penny's as he took in the lights and decorations piled high in her shopping cart. Looking at her at the Christmas market when shoving a cookie half into his mouth to keep from talking her out of yet another Santa purchase.

Looking at her as they loaded their bags into their respective vehicles and suggested they combine forces to get through all the holiday prep. Much like a couple would do.

Except they weren't a couple. And if the Christmas Beach busybodies thought there was more going on, well, they had their thinking all wrong.

Because if Jeff had been looking at her, it meant nothing.

Nothing at all.

FOUR

Maddie and Jeff arrived home from church at the same time. He exited his truck and raised a hand, then fluttered his tie. "Let me change and I'll be over."

She waved back, glad to have a few minutes to breathe and check that the food hadn't failed her. The moment she turned her key in the kitchen door lock, she knew it hadn't.

The smells of seasoned beef and vegetables

wafting through the room set her stomach to growling, reminding her how little she'd eaten this morning. Little, because after starting the slow cooker, she'd scurried around straightening up the living room and cleaning the kitchen... for a man who'd been inside countless times over the years.

A man who'd seen her house clean. Seen it dirty.

Seen her house on fire. Seen it under construction.

He probably wouldn't even notice.

She couldn't get Lisa's comments out of her mind. They hadn't talked after services; Lisa had been whisked away by one of Chelsea's high school teachers for lunch. They'd invited Maddie to join them. All she'd said when she declined was that she had a pot roast in the slow cooker calling her name.

She wasn't about to mention Jeff would share it with her.

How *did* Jeff look at her? According to Lisa, she was the only one oblivious.

And what would Lisa say about the way Maddie looked at him?

In her bedroom, she exchanged her sweater and dress pants for a long-sleeved T-shirt, jeans, and tennis shoes. By the time she made it back to the kitchen, she heard Jeff's steps on the back porch. He opened the door, saying, "Knock, knock."

"I'm here," she called from the pantry where a stray thought had sent her to check for a can of pumpkin. Alex loved her mother's pumpkin chiffon pie. She didn't know if she'd have time to make one, but at least she didn't need to buy pumpkin.

She pulled in a deep breath to settle nerves that the sound of Jeff's voice had stirred to life. What in the world was going on here? This was Jeff, her neighbor, her friend.

Yes, her feelings for him had deepened over time, growing roots and involving her heart. But he was still Jeff.

Just Jeff.

"Wow," he said, closing the door on a rush of crisp cool air and walking into the room. "Something smells great."

She stopped at the table to add the pie crust to her shopping list, then looked over. In place of his white dress shirt and tie, he now wore a black button-down with white pinstripes. He still wore his suit pants and dress shoes.

She felt decidedly underdressed but convinced herself he'd been in too big of a hurry to change more than he had. Besides, getting out of dress clothes was the first thing she did when she got home, no matter where she'd worn them. She blamed the fact that she'd been wearing scrubs to work her entire adult life.

She hated structured clothing. "Did you grow up eating Sunday pot roast?"

"Not that smelled like yours," he said, stirring the nerves he'd missed the first time.

Silly nerves. Silly stomach. If she didn't calm down, she'd never be able to eat. "Or maybe you were too young to notice."

"I would've noticed."

This time, the nerves tingled from a place near her heart. "It's probably the slow cooker. Seriously. It's foolproof. Everything falls to pieces, and I use a seasoning packet, so there's no wondering if I've forgotten one thing or another."

Jeff was looking behind the pot at the connection to the wall. "And it's safe to leave cooking while you're gone?"

"That's the point. That's how they're made. Yes."

"So no fire hazard."

"That was one time," she said, holding up one finger. "And not my fault."

"I know. Just hard to leave the job at the station."

"Uh-huh."

He shoved his hands in his pockets and shrugged. "Want some help?"

"Do you mind if we dish up at the counter? I know it makes me a terrible hostess—"

"No. It makes you practical. If I were at home, I might just eat straight out of the pot." He shrugged again. "Single life. What can I say?"

Rather than giving voice to any of the things floating around in her head, things that edged too close to flirting when he was here as a friend, she opened the cabinet door above the slow cooker and handed him two plates. Then she pulled open the drawers with utensils and serving spoons. "You want to do the food while I get our drinks?"

"Sure thing."

"Water or tea or soda? Or I can make coffee."

"Water's fine." He lifted the lid from the slow cooker, and Maddie heard his stomach growl. "Can I come back for seconds?"

"Of course," she said with a laugh. "Did you skip breakfast?"

"Sort of." He scooped out vegetables onto

both plates. "I was running late and downed a left-over biscuit with my coffee on the drive."

Sounded like Alex, she mused, pulling out her chair. Jeff brought over the plates and took the seat opposite. Alex's seat. Though when Jeff had eaten with them in the past, Alex had sat at the table's head. That he had still warmed Maddie's heart.

Jeff dug in while Maddie remained lost in thought. She wondered how he'd handled sending two kids to college at the same time. He'd never said much about missing them, about rambling around in his empty nest the way she'd done now for four months.

She knew he had. Of course he had. Those girls had been his life—

"Are you not hungry?" he finally asked, bringing her back.

She picked up her fork. "Just wondering how old that biscuit was you called breakfast."

He laughed, getting back to his food as Maddie started on hers. "I brought it home from the station on Friday. I'd intended to eat it on the drive, then Ashley called. I forgot it was in my truck until I was on my way to church."

Maddie gave him a look. "You ate a two-day-old biscuit on the way to church?"

He shrugged. "The coffee was fresh."

"Jeff Murphy." She shook her head, forking up a bite of shredded meat. "What am I going to do with you?"

Her question hung in the air above them. She wanted to reach up and snatch it back. It was something she'd say to Alex. And it was okay that she'd said it to Jeff.

But ever since Penny's and the Christmas market, and after Lisa's comments at church, well, she was having a lot of trouble walking the tightrope between their last two decades and her newly realized rush of feelings.

She didn't want to give him the wrong idea.

Unless it was the right idea.

Ugh.

He cleared his throat, a sort of light chuckle. "Keep feeding me?"

"In that case, let's talk menus."

She reached for the legal pads, sliding one toward him and moving hers closer. This was why they were here. Not to flirt, if that's what they were doing, though she knew it wasn't. It couldn't be. It was the same friendly banter they always whipped back and forth. Really. Who ate a biscuit that had been sitting in a truck for two days?

Feeling lighter, she reached for her pen. "Can you talk and eat at the same time?"

"Depends on if you want me to talk with my mouth full."

She rolled her eyes. "Between bites would be great."

"Sure. Let's do it."

"Okay," she said, taking a deep breath. This was just Jeff. "Let's start with the obvious must-haves and favorites."

He nodded. His mouth was full again.

"Turkey or ham?"

"Ashley usually does turkey. Audrey does ham except when she does lasagna, but that's only when her in-laws are coming. Sometimes we end up with all three."

"Do you want all three?" Because that was a lot of food. Lasagna meant garlic bread and salad. Turkey meant dressing, ham, sweet potato casserole...

"We could eat it, but I want what's easy."

"Lasagna, not so much. At least if you're wanting it from scratch. I mean, it's not hard. It's just more involved. Turkeys are pretty simple depending on the brine."

"Brine."

"Brine. Ham is probably the least labor intensive. But probably the priciest."

"What do you make?"

"Dr. Belton gives us all a gift certificate for Christmas, and I spend it on a ham. So I'll bring that. You decide on turkey or lasagna. Or both. But turkeys will go fast and you're going to need a pretty big one, so don't waffle too long."

"Waffles sound good."

"I'll put them on the breakfast menu." She flipped to a clean sheet and titled it BREAKFAST, then jotted the word, adding butter and syrup to a third page titled SHOPPING. After a moment, she added waffle mix. "Do you have a waffle iron? Or does Santa need to bring you one of those, too?"

Laughing, he shoved more food into his mouth. Then he looked up, confused, as if realizing she was only halfway kidding. "I have a toaster."

"You can use mine," she said, laying aside her pen and eating most of her vegetables while her mind clicked through her lists, while it also drifted to Lisa's comments from this morning. How *did* Jeff look at her? And how did she look at him?

"Moving on."

"Shoot."

"Do you have any special dishes everyone will want? Ones with ingredients neither of us will have on hand?" She picked up her pen. "And do you have the recipes?"

"If I don't, the girls will. What about you?"

"Sure. I grew up eating my grandmother's fudge and a cake of my mother's, a devil's food so rich it was nearly black." She smiled as she thought about it. "It has the most incredible icing. A white icing. But not vanilla, really. I can't explain it."

"Then you'll just have to make it so I'll better understand," he said, pushing back out of his chair and returning to the slow cooker.

She grinned. "It's Alex's favorite. He gets it every year on his birthday. I'll do it instead of the fudge. Lisa almost always brings me fudge, anyway."

He nodded and set about attacking his second plate while she jotted down what she could remember of the cake's ingredients. She should have most, but since Alex's birthday was in January, no reason not to buy the powdered sugar and cocoa, especially since Toussaint's stocked an upmarket brand she liked to use.

She looked up to find Jeff studying her. He

reached for his napkin to wipe his mouth, then he said, "Deep thoughts?"

"Food. Traditions. What do you eat for your birthday?"

"Depends on who's doing the cooking."

"You don't have a favorite birthday dish?"

"Summer birthday, so usually barbecue. But growing up it was always my gran's tamales."

That surprised her. "Tamales. Really."

"Yep. From scratch, though usually out of the freezer. I mean, she didn't make them fresh for my birthday. She would just put on a huge Tex-Mex spread."

"Was she from Texas?" she asked, reaching for her water glass and thinking she hadn't eaten Tex-Mex in ages.

Jeff nodded. "Met my granddad there when he was working as a roughneck. Work brought them here, and they stayed. She was an amazing cook."

Maddie studied his face, the smile brought on by memories. "I didn't know any of that about you."

He thought for a minute, pushing away his empty plate. "If we talk about family, it's usually about our kids. I mean, I've met your sister and her bunch. They visited once at Memorial Day.

The girls and I came and ate burgers with all of you."

"I remember."

"I could eat more of those burgers."

Maddie was pretty sure he could eat anything. "I'll have to get her husband's recipe. We can add that to your menu. A cookout is always fun."

"As long as you and Alex come."

"I've never known my son to turn down burgers."

"Great. It's settled."

"Now," she said, focusing them again. They'd be here all day at this rate... which, she had to admit, she wouldn't mind. He was so easy to be with, to talk to. She'd enjoyed no one's company more. The thought tangled with Lisa's lingering comments, leaving her stomach in knots. "Can we settle the rest of the Christmas menu?"

"Sure," he said as he got up to carry his dishes to the sink. He glanced back. "Want anything while I'm up?"

"I'm fine, thanks." She ate a bite of pot roast. Then ate another. It really was good. "I just need to know about any other must-haves."

He settled into his chair before he answered. "My mom's cranberry salad. I'll dig up the recipe for you, if I can figure out where I buried it, but I know it's fresh cranberries, fresh red grapes, whipping cream, and chopped nuts. Something else, but it's been a while since I've watched Ashley throw it together."

"Ashley."

"Audrey never was a fan. Ashley couldn't get enough. Still can't."

Maddie added the ingredients to the list titled CHRISTMAS. "I can probably Google the recipe. Seems all the secret family recipes are now online."

"Kinda takes away the anticipation. No need to wait for Mom to bring a bowl at Christmas. I can have it on my phone in seconds. If I cooked. Or made food things."

She laughed. The man would cook like a pro by the time Christmas arrived. "Do you think that? About anticipation?"

"Maybe. A little bit. I dunno," he said, wrapping both hands around his water glass and looking down. "There's something about having to wait. Instant gratification isn't always a good thing. I mean, frozen pizzas, sure," he said, and Maddie sputtered.

Then he pulled out his phone. "Do you have any family favorites?"

She nodded, thinking of one of the best. "My mom's banana cake. It's actually the icing that makes it. A sort of brown sugar fudge. It's my favorite part. It's everyone's favorite part."

He held his phone to his mouth. "Banana cake with brown sugar fudge icing recipe."

"Funny." But then he turned the screen to show her all the options. She took it out of his hand and clicked through several, scrolling to the bottom of the posts where the ingredients were always listed. She handed back the phone. "Close, but no cigar."

"Do you make it for Christmas?" he asked, returning his phone to his pocket.

It was such a man motion, leaning to one side, straightening one leg, shoving the phone into place before sitting straight again. She took a deep breath. "Not usually."

"Bummer. I love banana bread. Sounds like this might be even better."

"I've got a great banana bread recipe, too."

"Want me to ask Google about that one?"

"I do not," she said, adding bananas to her shopping list and putting a numeral two next to the brown sugar while Jeff laughed. "It's not funny."

"You're funny."

She ignored that and got back to Christmas. Ignored, too, the prickles of heat her pulse raised on her skin. "Does your family like cornbread dressing or traditional stuffing or some other variation? Sausage? Oyster?"

"Cornbread and that's Ashley's domain."

"Perfect," Maddie said. "She might want to double it so there will be enough for Alex."

"Note to self. Tell Ashley she'll need to quadruple the cornbread dressing."

"Especially if you want leftovers."

"Are you kidding? Leftovers are the best part of Christmas dinner. Oh, and that cranberry salad?" He shook his head and made a mm-mm-mm sound. "Pour that on the dressing and smother it all in gravy and that right there, my dear, is heaven."

My dear.

It meant nothing. A simple address that held no more meaning than if he'd said *my friend*. She wished he'd said *my friend*.

Because now she was going to waste time wondering if it wasn't so simple at all.

FIVE

Maddie was barely through the back door of Christmas Beach Pediatrics when her best friend, Tammy Hester, stepped into her path. She put the tablet she held into sleep mode, then looked up, her questioning gaze demanding Maddie's attention.

"Good morning to you too," Maddie said as the door latched, and she juggled her bags to shrug out of her hoodie.

Tammy wrapped both arms around the tablet and held it to her chest. "My mother said she saw you at the Christmas market on Saturday."

Your mother and Rose Foster, and how many others? "We can still go next weekend. You know I can't resist finding Santas on sale."

But Tammy ignored that and went on. "She said she saw you there with Jeff Murphy."

"Yep," Maddie said, taking off down the short hallway and leaving Tammy to follow. She needed another cup of coffee and to scan the list of the day's appointments before the clinic opened. "We ran into each other at Penny's and realized we weren't having any luck finding what we wanted, so we tried the market instead."

"Jeff Murphy, Maddie."

Maddie dropped her bags on the break room table and looked up. Tammy's dark brows rose. Her dark eyes waited. She was Maddie's height, Maddie's size, Maddie's age, but somehow Maddie felt chastised. Best friends were supposed to share the nitty-gritty of their relationships, their dates, their love lives with each other.

That's what she was reading in Tammy's expression.

But Tammy would wait a really long time since

none of those described Maddie's friendship with Jeff. She hooked her hoodie on the corner coatrack and stored her lunch in the fridge. Her purse went into her locker.

Once all of that was done, she grabbed her mug from the dishwasher and set it on the Keurig machine. She watched the mug fill as she spoke. "He's my neighbor, Tammy. I've known him... wow. I've known him more than half my life."

With a sigh, Tammy shook her head and checked a notification on her smart watch. "I don't know why you two haven't gotten together before now."

"We're not together now." Maddie's reminder was insistent. And as much for herself as for her friend, especially in light of Lisa's similar comment from yesterday. "We're neighbors."

"Based on what Crissy Cochrane said when I picked up Dane from her house Saturday night—"

"Why are you listening to anything Crissy Cochrane says?" Maddie asked as she brought her mug to her mouth and blew across the surface. The steam curled and rose, warming her face, smelling like the best part of the morning.

Tammy set her tablet on the table and dropped into a blue plastic chair. She crossed her legs and crossed her arms and stared Maddie down. "Because she knows everything about everybody?"

"Uh-huh," Maddie muttered as she joined her, sliding the tablet close and swiping the screen to life. She navigated to the appointment calendar.

"Are you saying you didn't go shopping with Jeff Murphy?"

"I'm saying don't listen to Crissy or anyone about this." There wasn't an empty appointment slot left in the day. It was going to be a long one. An exhausting one. "Yes, Jeff and I went shopping and we'll probably be doing it again."

"Oh?"

Maddie slid the tablet back toward Tammy. "His entire family is coming for a week, and I lost all my lights and ornaments in the fire, so we were doing some commiserating along with buying out Penny's and the market."

"You sure that's all you were doing?" Tammy asked as she checked her watch again.

Maddie ignored the image of Jeff hovering in her kitchen and changed the subject when Tammy shook her head and groaned. "Everything okay?"

"Dane left his algebra homework on the floor in the living room where he supposedly finished it *while* playing video games. I can't go get it and he can't reach his dad. I suppose this is going to end up being a lesson in responsibility. And priorities."

"And he's not even a teenager yet."

"Don't remind me. Next time I have kids, I'll do it when I'm a lot younger. And have a lot more energy and patience."

Maddie wanted to laugh but knew Dane had given Tammy more trouble in the last year than Maddie had ever had to deal with from Alex.

Some of that was just different dispositions. No two kids were ever the same. But Tammy's husband had decided he was in love with someone else and moved out two years ago.

It had been a tough time for both Tammy and her son, Maddie knew, finishing her coffee and washing her mug. Then she unscrewed the top of a bottle of water and downed half of it. When Tammy rolled her eyes, she said, "Hey, I saw today's schedule. We'll be lucky to get ten minutes for lunch. And hydration is your friend."

"Hydration... and Jeff Murphy?"

And Maddie had been so close to escaping. "Really?"

"C'mon. Throw your bestie a bone. The truth from the horse's mouth." Tammy's mouth twisted.

"If only to keep me from digging up more animal clichés."

Maddie gave up the fight. "He came over for lunch after church yesterday. He needed help to plan meals for the week after Christmas and to make sure he had kid-friendly groceries on hand for his grandkids."

"Seems like something their moms could take care of."

"Yeah, maybe, but we kind of bartered an exchange of services," she said, realizing that was one shopping list they hadn't made—what do the grandkids eat?

"I see."

"I need help with my outdoor lights. Alex always did them," she said, realizing that wasn't precisely true. "I mean, Jeff helped in the past before Alex took over, but with the fire, I'll feel better having another pair of eyes on the tree."

"Especially since his belong to a firefighter."

"Exactly."

At that, Tammy cackled. "You're hilarious, you know that?"

"So I've been told."

"Why don't you two just get all the garbage out of the way and get together already?"

"What garbage?"

"Whatever's keeping you apart."

"There's nothing keeping us apart," she said and frowned because that sounded like there was no reason for them not to get together. "I mean, we're happy being friends. We've always been great friends. Why mess up a good thing when..."

"When?"

When I don't know if he feels the same about me as I do about him.

There. She'd said it. Or thought it at least. It didn't matter how deep for Jeff her love ran if the love was one-sided. If he didn't want their relationship to change.

And she wasn't about to ask him. So she supposed the status quo would remain.

"When I don't have time for anything in my life right now but Alex coming home for the holidays and work."

✶✶✶✶✶✶✶✶✶✶✶✶✶

"Any chance you're heating leftovers for supper?"

"Actually, yes," Maddie said, having heard Jeff's

steps on the gravel driveway. His steps. Not those of another neighbor or a Christmas caroler or a delivery driver bringing any of her Christmas gift orders to the door. She knew Jeff's steps the same way she knew her son's. She accepted the familiarity for the truth it was, looked toward him, and sighed. "Would you like to join me?"

"Depends on what that sigh means."

"It means I'm tired and I'm starving."

"Well, let's get you fed."

Jeff was dressed in dark jeans, a navy polo with the CBFD logo, and wore a navy ball cap with the same. "I've been thinking about your pot roast since last night. I even told the girls Santa could bring me a slow cooker if he was so inclined."

A grin broke across Maddie's face, lightening her steps, her mood, the load of stress she'd been carrying since, well, since Alex had left for college in August. He had three and a half more years of college. After that, depending on finances and everything facing young adults these days, he'd be on his own.

She needed to get used to being on hers. "What did they say?"

He dug his phone from his pocket to show her the messages. She took it and handed him her door keys. Audrey had sent a group text to him and Ashley with links to five options that would feed a crowd of ten or a single person.

Maddie laughed. "A single person. Like one person? Or one unmarried person? I mean, what if a married person wanted to prepare a single meal?"

He pushed open her door and handed back her keys as she returned his phone. "You'll have to take that up with the marketing department."

She dropped her bags on the couch, switching on a second-floor lamp to add more light to the room than that from the one she'd scheduled to come on at the same time as the porch light. Using an electrical timer. One she hadn't run by Jeff.

Hmm. "At least the girls are on it."

"They're good about overwhelming me with choices."

"Meaning the anxiety of making one will keep you from doing so," she said as he followed her to the kitchen where she flipped on those lights too.

It was crazy how early it got dark this time of year. How she almost never saw daylight, except on the weekends, unless she went out for lunch.

It was also crazy how natural it felt to have Jeff in her kitchen, both still in work clothes, her scrubs navy, her clogs striped in multiple hues of blue.

He'd been here a lot over the years, but until four months ago, Alex had always been here too. They'd talked fires and football and her son had been a buffer.

Now it was just her and Jeff. Her and Jeff and their plans for Christmas, and all the things she felt that she'd worked hard to keep at bay.

Was this the garbage Tammy was talking about?

Ugh.

"Oh," he said, retrieving his phone again. Hers dinged moments later with a text. "That's a pic of the cranberry salad recipe. For the shopping list."

"So it wasn't buried somewhere?"

"No. It's buried. I got that from Ashley."

Maddie arched a brow. "I think that's cheating."

"It's how I'm surviving middle age."

"Ha," she said, opening the fridge. "You know I haven't stopped thinking about that since you mentioned it, for which I do *not* thank you."

"You're welcome, anyway."

She set the serving bowls of food on the counter. "I'd always thought middle age was how the young-uns thought of us. Not how we'd eventually think of ourselves."

"I still think of myself as the man I was when."

Maddie waited for more but realized that was all he was going to say. And she laughed, reaching up to take two plates out of the cabinet. "You okay with filling your plate, then nuking it?"

"Isn't that one of the rules of middle age?"

Rules? Really? "I hadn't even realized I *was* middle-aged until you dropped that bomb in Penny's."

"Sorry," he said, taking the plate she handed him, then nodding at her to fill hers first. "If it helps, I've never thought of you that way."

Her serving spoon hovered over the potatoes and carrots. Her hand shook. "I've never thought of you that way, either."

"Just as long as you think of me."

She didn't look over. She couldn't look over. It was a miracle she was able to get the food onto her plate without splattering it across the counter.

She scrambled for something to say that wasn't too flippant or leading. That wasn't flirtatious. She settled on the truth. "Every time I plug something into the wall."

"Funny," he said with a gut-deep laugh, and the surrounding tension went up in smoke. So, to speak.

Maddie breathed in, handing him the spoon. "Your turn."

While she heated her food, he piled his plate high, vegetables around the edge, leaving a bowl for the meat in the middle. "Do you want to go tree shopping one night this week?"

She focused on her plate rotating in the microwave. The motion made her dizzy and tired. "I'll have to figure out when to fit it in."

"I can do it," he said, setting his plate aside and rinsing out both serving dishes in the sink. "I know what fits your space as well as mine."

It would be such a relief to have that one chore taken care of for her. Alex had done it the last couple of years. Maddie was pretty sure his insistence had to do with which friends worked there. Especially which girls.

And if Jeff bought the trees, the gossip mill could churn on his need for two and leave her out of it. "Would you mind? I know you just offered..."

"I did. And I do not."

"I need lots of branches. *Lots* of branches."

"Yep. For lots of lights and lots of ornaments. I know," he said, setting his plate in the microwave. "I'll do it after work tomorrow."

"Can I pay you then? I don't have any cash on me."

"Don't worry about it. I can afford a tree."

She cringed. "Am I going to be able to afford you hanging my lights?"

"It's plugging them in that's gonna cost you," he said and smiled as the microwave dinged.

Six

They had their Christmas Day menu and another for Jeff to work from for the week with his family. They had their shopping list, Jeff's near-empty freezer, and Maddie's second fridge in the garage.

Alex used that one for his sports and energy drinks, bottled water, and bags of oranges and apples. It had sat nearly empty for four months.

They also had Maddie's huge walk-in pantry. It

was one of her favorite things about the house. And keeping it stocked was one of her favorite things to do. It was like having a grocery store in her kitchen. She loved it. And okay. She had control issues.

Tonight, they'd both have trees to go with their copious decorations. After that, all that was left was to hang lights and wrap gifts. With all of Jeff's people coming for Christmas and their two families sharing the day, Maddie had quite a few left to buy.

For the big day, they'd use Jeff's formal serving dishes, once his mother's, along with the matching place settings for the adults.

There would be seven around his dining room table. The kids would use his everyday dishes and sit at a folding table in the same room. The tables would be covered by matching tablecloths. They were red and green plaid. They were Maddie's. And both were machine washable.

Maddie had offered her kitchen chairs should Jeff find he was short, but he'd counted and was pretty sure he had everyone covered. His dining room was larger than hers, and the floor being hardwood meant easy kid cleanup.

Everything was set. Almost. Mostly.

Now they needed to shop. And then they needed to cook. Cooking would take up a lot more of their time. Time they had to find after work and during the weekend hours that remained.

Part of Maddie was panicking even while she knew her lists, schedules, and calendars meant they were in decent shape. She was obsessive about keeping them updated. They gave her the same sense of control her stocked pantry did.

Another part of her was panicking because she would do it all with Jeff. And that was the panic that didn't come with lists, schedules, and calendars. It left her feeling anxious and completely out of control.

But the biggest part of her was panicking because she didn't want the menu planning and shopping and cooking and lights and decorations and gift-wrapping to impede Christmas. Of Alex coming home. Of their first holiday since the fire.

She didn't want to let him down. She refused to let him down.

So she would just breathe in and breathe out and cut back on her caffeine.

Tonight, on her way home, she stopped at Toussaint's to pick up a few of the items on her personal shopping list. She wanted to put together at least one of Alex's favorite dishes. She figured if she worked those in with the decorating and wrapping, she wouldn't have to do much cooking while he was home. They'd have more time together.

She thought about that for a moment, fishing her phone from her purse after setting it in the child seat of the grocery basket, and adding paper plates to her list. Having fewer dishes to do would free up even more of her time.

She also wanted to bake some cookies and freeze them and had only decided on that today.

Her mother had done that when she and her sister were young, baking a famous recipe without the called-for chocolate chips. Their family had gobbled them up as fast as they'd filled the freezer. They'd been just as good without the chocolate as with. And Alex absolutely loved them, grabbing them frozen just like she'd done so long ago.

She smiled at that as she maneuvered through the crowded aisles. Looked like she wasn't the only one making the most of her hours.

Carols played through the speakers and the cinnamon and spice smells coming from the in-store bakery had her stomach rumbling. She needed to get home and eat before she bought out the shelves.

After a quick chat with a couple of mothers of young patients, only one of whom mentioned Jeff, thank goodness, she pushed her basket up to the checkout lane and began unloading her items for scanning. Cookie ingredients returned her to her earlier thoughts.

She loved that she and her sister had carried on their mother's tradition. Maddie's two nieces might be even bigger plain cookie fans than Alex—

"Evening, Maddie," the cashier said, and Maddie looked up.

The older woman appeared exhausted. Wiry gray hair had escaped the severe bun at the back of her head. The store's harsh lights washed out her already ashen skin, emphasizing the deep creases at the corner of her eyes and around her lips. They were dry, what color she'd applied earlier long since chewed away.

"Hey, Jean." Maddie offered her a big smile. "How've you been?"

Jean Dow shrugged as she ran bags of sugar, flour, chopped nuts, and chocolate chips over the scanner. "This time of year my bursitis likes to make itself known."

"I'll bet," Maddie said, looking at the peanut butter she didn't remember adding to her cart. Oh, she must've been thinking about another of Alex's favorite treats, a chocolate no-bake cookie. Did she have enough butter? Enough cocoa and oatmeal? If so, she'd mix up a triple batch and bring a tin to Jean later in the month.

Bursitis. Right. "All that repetitive motion must aggravate it. I'm so sorry."

"It is what it is," the older woman said, frowning at Maddie's three bunches of overripe bananas. "Is Jeff with you tonight?"

Maddie's hands stilled. She blinked down at the extra bag of brown sugar that she probably wouldn't even open—the icing for her banana cake didn't need *that* much—as heat bloomed in her cheeks. "Jeff? Murphy? Why would he be with me?"

Lisa and Tammy were obviously right. The grapevine had decided this was the year to pair her and Jeff like some sort of fruit and cheese. Maybe she'd been more apparent than she'd realized with her feelings, wearing them on her sleeve.

Ugh.

Had Jeff noticed? She was going to have to be more careful.

Horse. Barn door.

Maddie sighed and tossed the brown sugar onto the belt.

"Heard the two of you've been doing a lot of your shopping together."

She waved a hand, doing her best to dismiss Jean's curiosity. "A onetime thing. Or a one-day thing. We ran into each other at Penny's, then thought we might have better luck at the Christmas market."

Jean didn't comment but continued to run Maddie's items over the scanner, bagging them as she went. She set another full sack on the counter and open the next on the standing rack. "Looks like you've got a lot of baking ahead of you."

Yes, but not for Jeff. At least not all. "Alex is finishing up his first semester of college. I haven't bought groceries like this since he left in August."

"He must have quite the appetite," Jean said, punching in the code for the cranberries and grapes. "Especially for fruit."

"He's nineteen. Comes with the territory. Banana bread, banana cake. Bananas," Maddie heard herself admitting, glancing at the two quarts of whipping cream she hadn't even registered adding. Wow. She'd either worked too hard today or slept too little last night, or she was running on autopilot.

And Jeff was mapping out her route.

Oh, good grief.

She looked at Jean then and added some truth to the rumors. Because why not? She and Jeff had nothing to hide and Jean, well, maybe it would lift her spirits to be the first to know. "Jeff and I are actually combining forces this year since his entire family is coming home. He's helping me hang my lights and I'm helping him cook."

"Thought he always hung your lights."

Maddie gave Jean the point. "He did for a while. Until Alex was old enough. But after last year, I'll be a lot more comfortable if someone else plugs them in."

"That's right. I'd forgotten about the fire." Jean stepped around the end of the counter for a free basket and loaded in Maddie's bags. Once she was done, she handed Maddie a candy cane. And a smile. "Hope this year goes better. And you stay safe."

"Thanks, Jean," Maddie said, returning her debit card to her wallet and waiting for her receipt. Jeff had insisted on reimbursing her for anything she bought for his recipes, but she would not accept his money. She did accept Jean's candy cane, though.

She'd crush it up and drop it into a mug of hot tea to go with the cookies she'd eat tonight, no chocolate chips and fresh out of the oven.

Jeff drove into his driveway as Maddie was unloading the rear of her SUV. He jogged across the street and took the bags she shoved against his chest.

"Sorry. I'll pick up the trees tomorrow night. Got tied up this afternoon thanks to a driver and the cigarette he threw into a ditch. You'd think people would use common sense..." He got a look at her face then and paused. "Guess you've heard the rumors."

She was certain her expression was foul. Whatever good will she'd felt toward Jean earlier had dissipated on the drive home, though she wasn't sure she knew why. "At church on Sunday. At work on Monday. Tonight at Touissant's."

"Wow. Wonder what tomorrow will bring?"

"Considering I gave Jean even more to chew on while checking out—"

"That would be why her husband asked me about it. About us."

"She didn't waste any time," Maddie said, the word *us* bouncing around her head. It was making her dizzy. "Where did you see Wallace?"

"He stops by the station for coffee once in a while. Likes to catch up with friends. Retirement isn't exactly doing him any favors."

Maddie blew out a defeated breath. "Jean didn't look good. Tired. I think I'll take them some cookies next week. If I get through my baking schedule."

"That'd be nice. They'd appreciate it I know." And then he stopped. "If helping with my cooking is going to slow your baking, I'll be fine. The girls will be here. They can manage what I can't."

"You mean if I will not have time to make my iced shortbread cookies—"

"Those would be the ones. I'm happy to eat frozen pizza every night. The family's here as long as I can have those cookies for dessert."

They were probably her favorite cookies in the world and more labor intensive with all the rolling and cutting and drizzling multiple colors of icing she then had to collect off waxed paper and try not to put into her mouth instead of into the bowl to drizzle again.

"I can do both. I can do it all. I can do anything."

"Because you're a comic book character with spider-bite powers?"

"I wish. Well, not the spider bite part."

He hefted another of her bags into his arms. "And that pep talk? About doing it all?"

"Helps to have a fan club."

"I'll be your fan club," he said, not a hint of teasing in his tone. He was being honest. He was being true.

It occurred to her then, as she turned to grab her purse and satchel from the passenger seat, leaving Jeff to close the cargo hatch, that hiding Santa's presents from a young Alex had been a piece of cake compared to how hard it was hiding her feelings from Jeff. Her palms were sweating. Her nape, beneath her hoodie, was sweating. Winter would officially arrive in less than three weeks.

So why was she sweating?

Just because Jeff had said he'd be her fan club?

It was obvious she needed more sleep, she

mused, locking up her SUV and heading for the back door. More sleep. Less gossip. More cookies. Less... Jeff following her, carrying her groceries, setting the bags on the kitchen table.

Making himself at home. In her home.

No matter how much she loved that he did.

"Hey, you bought cranberries. And grapes. And whipping cream. And nuts," he said, unloading each item. Then he reached into the next bag. "And bananas. Like... bananas!"

His excitement doused her crabby mood. Why did she care what Jean or Tammy and her mother or even Lisa's extensive circle of friends thought about her relationship to Jeff? Her relationship *with* Jeff? Because that was more accurate, wasn't it?

This past week—and it hadn't even been a week, more like four days—something had changed. In her, sure. That much she'd accepted. But he was different too...

She'd known him for half of her life and couldn't remember him ever being so... jolly. Was it just the season? Anticipating the arrival of his girls and their families? She was certainly drowning in holiday spirit, waiting for Alex to get home.

But there was a tension that belonged just to

her and Jeff. Not Alex. Not Ashley or Audrey. Not even to Santa Claus. And she was so afraid it was going to snap.

"I'm going to do as much baking to freeze as I can on Saturday. The banana bread takes a lot of cooking time, so I want to have that out of the way."

"Want some help? I can peel the bananas."

"Thanks. Because I wasn't sure I'd be able to handle that on my own."

Jeff grinned. "How about I do them after I hang the lights?"

"Oh." Yes. Please. Thank you. She hadn't wanted to bug him about that. He was as busy as she was. "Are you sure? You haven't hung your own yet."

"Rick Tracer's coming by on Friday to help me. We're both working the early shift."

"No reciprocal light hanging?"

Jeff chuckled. "He moved into an apartment and said he hung a string on his balcony and missed all the ladder climbing and aching back and shoulders."

"Now you're just trying to make me feel guilty."

"Let me peel the bananas and you're off the hook."

"Is it really about peeling the bananas?" she asked, looking into the fridge and waiting for a dinner idea to jump out at her. When nothing did, she closed the door and turned. "Or being here for the first batch that comes out of the oven?"

He pressed his hand to his heart. "You got me."

"It's probably only fair that I warn you." She leaned back against the fridge.

Jeff frowned and crossed his arms. "About?"

"I bought way too many lights this year."

"I know. I was in Penny's. I saw."

Maddie scrunched up her nose. "I'd already bought a few others before I bought those."

One of Jeff's brows went up. "How many is a few?"

"A lot."

"I see," he said, scratching his end-of-day face scruff.

"You don't have to hang them all."

"Yes, I do."

"I don't need them all."

"Yes, you do."

She narrowed her gaze, her skin warming as her pulse began to race. "How do you know?"

"Your subconscious was obviously making up for last year. And this year is all about making up for last year."

He left her breathless. How could he be so attuned to what she was feeling when she hadn't spoken of it at all? "Is it?"

"Of course it is," he said, leaving it at that as if the logic was there waiting for her once she got past the tenderness in his tone.

"Well," she finally said, balling up the empty shopping bags he'd left on the table. "It would be nice if my subconscious had her own job and checking account. She's about to buy me out of house and home."

"What happened to giving me the receipts for my stuff?" He looked at the table. "Cranberries, grapes, nuts, whipping cream. Pretty sure those are all mine."

"Don't worry about it." She shrugged, the plastic bags now balled in her hands. "My subconscious can afford cranberry salad."

He snorted, shaking his head as he walked to the back door and opened it. "What am I going to do with you, Maddie Craig?"

He was gone before she could answer. Or breathe.

SEVEN

A nd that was how Maddie and Jeff spent their second Saturday in a row together, though this time by design, with purpose, and with no one ogling.

The day also came with brownies Tammy had brought her from a school fundraising bake sale. And with a Crock-Pot of baked potato soup.

She'd prepped it all Friday night and set the

timer, waking to the mouthwatering smells. The soup was one of Alex's favorite winter comfort foods. She'd never understood why it couldn't comfort him year-round the way it did her.

Jeff knocked on her back door around noon. He'd had errands to run, which gave her time to make sure the house was in order, the food was ready, and all the recipes and ingredients were lined up on the counter. She refused to get halfway through anything only to realize she was missing something. This way, she never did.

His schedule also gave her time to make sure she was ready, though she wasn't even sure what that meant. But the week had been a busy one, so many kids with seasonal maladies, and she'd felt better after an extra-long hot shower.

She'd dressed casually, a long-sleeved tee rather than something heavier that would get too hot with the oven going all day, along with jeans that had been washed so many times they were as comfy as sweats.

Since she'd be spending the day in the kitchen, she opted for a topknot to keep her hair out of the way. And she chose shoes that would keep her feet from aching.

Like those of a middle-aged person.

"I sound like a broken record, but that smells amazing," Jeff said, leaning close to the slow cooker and pulling in a deep breath. "And I'm pretty sure I need to fill up on it before I start peeling bananas. Or hanging lights."

Maddie rolled her eyes. "It's going to kill you with carbs, so just be warned."

"Carbs and I go way back," he said, making himself at home and fetching two bowls from the cabinet and two spoons from the drawer. "One bowl of this and I'll have all the energy I need for the day."

She tried not to roll her eyes. Doing so made it too hard to watch him in her kitchen. "If you say so."

"What can I do? Grate cheese? Chop chives? Fry up some bacon?"

"Uh, who are you and what have you done with Jeff Frozen Pizza Murphy?"

"Just a man who has a thing for potato soup." He gave her a look she couldn't quite figure out. "And who raised two daughters without starving them."

"Ah, yes, necessity." Been there and done that. "And grated cheese would be nice. Chives too."

"And bacon?" he asked as he pulled open the fridge.

"Sure." She grinned, her heart growing several sizes, seeing as how it was the season for that sort of thing. "It'll delay eating—"

"But it will be worth every salty, crackly crunch." He tossed a pound of bacon to the stovetop, then dug out a frying pan. "I can put out your tree lights while it cooks."

She watched him get to work, kinda loving it, kinda in awe. "Most of the strands are multicolored, though I splurged on some strands of red, green, and white."

"Want me to string the colored ones first, then go back with the others?"

She looked on as he set the bacon to cook. "I dunno. Maybe save those. I'll return them. My subconscious has been wrong."

He turned to her after washing his hands and grinned. "Show me what you've got."

Thirty minutes later, they sat together at her

kitchen table, bowls of potato soup steaming in front of them. Maddie sprinkled cheese, chives, and bacon on top of hers, passing each to Jeff as she did. "Did you cook growing up?"

Focused on his soup, Jeff shrugged. "Some. Stuff on the grill. My mother made sure I knew how to do more with eggs than boil them, which was great because the girls lived on them for the first few months after..."

After their mother left. He didn't need to finish the sentence. "Eggs are good. Easy."

He spooned up a bite of soup and blew across it. "I used to cook off and on at the firehouse so I could manage spaghetti, chili mac, stuff like that. Like I said, carbs and I go way back, and the girls were big fans."

Maddie said nothing. She loved hearing him tell stories—he rarely said anything more about himself than how his day had gone—so focused on eating while he talked.

"But then word of my divorce got around," he said with a snort. "And suddenly my freezer was full of casseroles."

Maddie nearly choked, imagining that string of cars. "I'll bet it was."

Another snort, but no other response. He wore

a deep frown, as if his admission had taken him back to a place he didn't want to go. "To be honest, I was glad to get them. I had a full-time job, a monster of a house to manage, and two little girls looking at me like they were scared to death they'd wake up the next morning and find me gone too."

Maddie's heart clutched as the air in the room stilled. Not once, in twenty years, had Jeff said a word about what he'd gone through in those early days of finding himself an unexpected single parent. Not about the worry or the responsibility. He'd only mentioned his divorce twice and then in passing.

She didn't move. She wanted to hear more, to learn more. To know more and know him better. She wanted to understand him, good and bad and in-between.

She loved him.

After a moment, he went on. "They both slept with me for a while. Probably a year. I didn't encourage it, but I didn't say no. I couldn't say no. And honestly, I loved lying there in the dark, listening to them breathe. I had the worst insomnia. I think I was afraid I'd wake up, and they were the ones who'd be gone too."

Two short revelations. About his feelings.

About his girls. Not a word about his ex... as if she'd never existed. And except for the daughters she'd given him, Maddie could imagine it seeming that way to him. To Audrey and Ashley too.

Maddie had heard the gossip, of course. His ex hadn't wanted kids. The pregnancy had been an accident. And she certainly didn't want to be saddled with two, raising them in a town the size of Christmas Beach where she couldn't even get her hair highlighted right.

The pain of all that hurt and loss nearly gutted Maddie. Poor babies. Her heart broke again for Jeff's girls. For Jeff too. Their lives as single parents had been so different, their challenges so similar, yet their grief completely their own.

Her vision blurred, her eyes teary. She didn't know what to say.

She took two bites of her soup before she looked up, knowing from Jeff's expression that she didn't need to say anything at all. He saw what she was feeling.

Every single bit of what she was feeling.

He set down his spoon and cleared his throat. "Ready to plug in the lights?"

She nodded.

Jeff stood and carried their bowls and spoons to the counter, leaving them next to the slow cooker. He set the cheese, chives, and bacon in the fridge. Then he came back and offered her his hand. She took it. It was warm and engulfed hers with its size and strength. She never wanted him to let her go.

He led her through the house to the living room. That was when he released her, saying, "You sure you want me to do it?"

She nodded again. Then she moved to stand facing the tree, taking in the distance that would show her all the lights. A distance that allowed her to see Jeff.

He knelt behind the tree. The strings were connected one to the next, leaving a single plug at the end. He had equipped her with a surge protector that offered additional outlets in case she required them, and he had incorporated a foot pedal to enable her to switch them on and off effortlessly.

He held the plug in one hand. "Here we go."

The tree exploded in colors, bursts of red and green and white, blue and yellow, even softer purple and orange and pink. It was glorious. It was bright and beautiful and everything Christmas tree lights should be. And none of it was burning.

Jeff sat back on his heels and smiled. "And Merry Christmas to you!"

Maddie dropped cross-legged to the floor, buried her face in her hands, and sobbed.

"This is going to make a ton of banana things," Jeff said, his gaze traveling over the ingredients set out on the table. "Like almost literally."

After turning on the tree's lights, he'd left her to decorate while he hung the lights outside. She'd offered to come out and help. He'd told her that wasn't their deal.

And she hadn't planned to do the tree then; she had too much baking on the day's agenda. But seeing the lights shining across her new hardwood floor, reflecting off the glass of her framed photos of Alex, coloring the walls with twinkling bursts of all those colors, she hadn't been able to resist. She and her subconscious were definitely going to have a talk. She'd sorted through the ornaments they'd bought and set half of them aside to return. What a waste of time she didn't have.

Her overbuying wasn't that surprising, she mused, considering the food items she probably wouldn't even use this year. Most of those had a distant expiration date, and she'd use them long before then. But the decorations, and the extra lights, were all tied to the fire and that loss. She stopped beating up her subconscious.

Obviously, it was paying better attention to her emotional state than she was.

She looked at the table again. Jeff wasn't wrong. Her mother's banana muffin—or banana bread—recipe was wonderfully dense and moist. "We can both fill our freezers."

"Or our mouths," Jeff said, and she swore she heard his stomach rumble.

"Feel free to eat while you peel. I'll freeze what's left." If any were, she mused, as he found one that wasn't as brown as the others.

He broke it in half. "Do you remember that day, Alex was about three, I think, and he wasn't having anything to do with letting you unload the groceries?"

Jeff had seen her juggling bags and trying to corral her son. He'd offered to wait outside with a rambunctious Alex while she got the door unlocked and her frozen items into the house. "By the time I came back for him, he'd eaten three of the bananas from the bunch I'd just bought for the week."

"We shared one of those," Jeff said.

Maddie snorted out a laugh while hefting her mixer to the counter. "Knowing what I do about you now, that doesn't surprise me."

"I don't think I ever told you," he said, frowning, hesitant, his hands messy with banana. "That was the first time he called me Daddy."

Maddie's fingers on her mixer plug stilled. "The first time?"

"He did it a few. When he was pretty young."

She looked down, blowing out a slow steadying breath. Not once had she heard Alex call Jeff anything but Mr. Jeff. "I'm sorry. I didn't know."

"Maddie. There's nothing to apologize for." He pushed away from the table to wash his hands. Then he reached for her wrist and squeezed. "He knew that's what Audrey and Ashley called me. I'm sure he picked it up from them. No harm. No foul."

Maddie didn't know why this had stunned her. Three-year-olds didn't have it in them to grasp the complexities of families. "Did he ever ask about his own dad?"

Jeff took the cord from her hand and plugged in the mixer. "I don't think so."

"He doesn't even look like Rob. He looks just like me."

"And I got one of each, though Audrey's blond doesn't come from a salon." He added the last as he returned to the table.

Maddie waited for him to get settled before prying. "Do you see her? Their mother? When you look at them now?"

A grin took over his face, bright in his scruff. Bright, too, in his eyes. "Not at all. And it would be okay if I did, you know. But they're their own women. Strong and smart. So smart. I can't even tell you how proud I am of them."

"You're a great dad, Jeff. The girls are so lucky." She stopped herself from adding that Alex would've been lucky, too. Alex had been lucky. He was *still* lucky. Jeff had been the father figure he'd needed. He'd been there when her son couldn't come to her.

For that, she'd be eternally grateful.

The oven buzzed three times, letting her know it had reached temperature. And here she hadn't even started the mixer yet. "This day is *not* sticking to the plan."

Jeff glanced over at the oven, glanced up at her, then held out one hand in offering. "Banana?"

She rolled her eyes and got to work.

EIGHT

Christmas

Beach

"Finally!" Maddie exclaimed as the back door opened and Alex walked through.

She'd heard his truck tires crunch over the driveway's gravel and forced herself to finish loading the last three forks and mugs into the dishwasher. She'd fumbled the forks and nearly dropped a mug; her hands were trembling with such excitement.

She'd heard the slam of his door and the fob's

electronic chirp as he'd locked up and forced herself to add soap and start the machine. She'd managed that with only a bit of soap missing the dispenser. She'd wanted everything perfect when he arrived.

She didn't know why. He'd grown up in this house. Nothing had ever been perfect. He would not come home after four months and expect things to have changed. Except things *had* changed. With her. With Jeff. And she knew with Alex too.

His dark hair was longer than usual, a shock falling nearly to his eyes. He wore jeans, athletic shoes, and a sweatshirt emblazoned with his school's Falcon mascot. He looked so good. *So* good. Healthy. Well-rested. Older. Wiser. How did teen boys do it? Though in another few months, he'd roll over into his twenties.

Half of middle age.

She didn't even bother drying her hands but met him as he dropped his red-and-white school duffel to the floor. She wrapped him up as tightly as she could, her arms around his neck, his shoulders seeming so much wider than when she'd hugged him goodbye.

Where had her little boy gone? She sniffed back

the flood of emotion making her nose and eyes all goopy and wet. She wasn't ever letting him out of her sight again.

"I was about to send out a search party," she said, her heart thundering.

"One led by a red-nosed reindeer?" Alex asked as Maddie squeezed him once more as tightly as her arms could manage.

He was so tall and so very broad. When had he gotten so broad? "That reindeer is probably booked up for the night, but I imagine I can get my hands on a fire engine."

"Ha," he said, squeezing her just as tightly as she held on to him for another long moment. "Same as the last twenty years?"

She smacked him on the butt and stepped back. *Not the same at all* was what she wanted to say, but she didn't. She was still working out what magic this month had rained down on her and Jeff. Because something had happened.

Just nothing she wanted to talk about with her son. "Is it weird that we've lived across the street from one another for two decades?"

"Maybe a little bit. Or maybe not at all in Christmas Beach." He shrugged, stripping off his sweatshirt. He wore an old graphic tee he'd bought in high school, the LSU logo faded nearly to white. "The lights look great, by the way."

They did. All twenty gazillion of them. "Jeff hung them."

"I figured. I mean, he did them before I was able. Then supervised once I was tall enough—"

"And focused enough not to fall off the ladder."

"That too." He grinned.

She stepped back and searched his expression. "Are you sorry you grew up here?"

"Why would you ask me that?"

His frown was curious. She shook her head. "Just thinking of all the people you've met since leaving in August. All those different experiences."

"More than a few of them think it's pretty cool that I actually have a hometown. Few of them do. Or their town is ten times the size of Christmas Beach, so all they know is their own neighborhood." He reached down to unzip his duffel. "And I don't think any of them have a firefighter at their beck and call."

"Hilarious," she said before asking him the thing all moms asked. "Are you hungry?"

"Is Santa's beard white?" he replied as he stood

and handed her a gift box. "Merry Christmas, Mom."

"I thought we were going to exchange gifts in the morning," she said, her eyes misty.

"We are. This isn't that."

"Then what is it?" The paper was a metallic silver printed in flocked snowflakes. The bow on top reached from corner to corner and had small snowflakes tied into the knot.

His grin was full of dimples and cheer. "Probably need to open it to find out."

She pulled at the ribbon, then opened the flaps to find a snow globe nestled inside in tissue paper stamped with silver stars. The glass sphere sat on a wooden base. The figurine inside was of Santa's upper half, his lower half stuck in a chimney.

It was adorable. It was perfect.

It broke the dam holding back Maddie's emotions, and she began to sob. Huge, gulping, racking sobs.

"Mom!" Alex's expression grew distressed, his frown drawing a deep vee between his brows. "I didn't want you to cry!"

"Of course I'm going to cry. You just gave me a new snow globe. My first new snow globe of the year." She hadn't even bought any of those she'd seen at the Christmas Market. And she didn't know why. She gripped it to her chest. "Thank you."

"I know what your collection meant to you," he said, wrapping an arm around her and dropping a kiss to the top of her head.

"This one will mean even more. Thank you. Thank you. I love you. I'm so glad you're home. And never leave me again." She sniffed and stared down into the glass, shaking it and watching the snow settle. "At least not this year."

Alex laughed. "I love you too and you're welcome, but please don't cry."

"You might as well give up all hope in that regard. It's Christmas. You're here. And I have missed you like crazy."

"I've missed you too. But now for the important stuff."

"What's that?" she asked, shaking the globe again.

"Whaddya got to eat? Because I am pretty sure I smell gumbo."

Since Maddie had done so much cooking earlier in the month—since she and *Jeff* had done so much cooking—and since she and Alex would eat a lot of food from the freezer, she'd spent today preparing them a special Christmas Eve dinner. It wasn't part of any holiday tradition but comprised a bunch of Alex's favorite things.

The gumbo had been simmering, and the room smelled of paprika and cayenne and fresh cornbread. She'd made red beans in the slow cooker, and using frozen crawfish tails since fresh were out of season, fixed étouffée.

Alex helped Maddie set everything on the table she'd covered with a bright-red cloth. Small green hand towels served as napkins, and the translucent glass of their iced tea glasses was printed with red and green holiday bells.

Alex stared at the feast as if he didn't know where to begin. "I did not know how much I would miss your cooking."

"I have missed having you to cook for," she said, reaching for a cornbread muffin and splitting it for the butter. "I've eaten too many sandwiches and bowls of soup, though I did put a pot roast in the slow cooker a couple of Sundays ago."

"That sounds good too." Alex dished up rice

and covered half with beans, half with étouffée. He filled a soup bowl with gumbo and dug in, blowing across his spoon, then running out of patience and eating it. "Oh, oh, pitch, this is good. And hot."

"Jeff thought so," she said, not sure if she was dropping a hint or a bomb.

Alex set down his tea glass and stared. "You cooked for Jeff?"

She shrugged and waved her hand, blowing it off as nothing. "He's eaten with us before. Dozens of times. Hundreds probably."

"Yeah," he said, digging back into his food. "When I was here and sometimes Audrey and Ashley. Not when it was just you two."

Because until the girls had moved away and Alex had left for college, there had always been someone to act as a buffer. A chaperone even... not that they'd needed one, she assured herself. They were, after all, middle-aged.

She spooned up a bite of gumbo, blowing to help it cool. "We did some bartering this year. I needed help with the lights outside. And I wanted to make sure the tree lights wouldn't burn down the house."

"And what did you do for him? Besides pot

roast?" he asked, and then his face colored and he lifted a hand. "Never mind."

"Alex! Get your mind back into Christmas," she said, not sure whether to laugh or turn his same shade of red. "His girls are coming for a week with their families, so I helped him work out a menu and shop."

He nodded as if that was acceptable. "Fair enough."

"And we're having Christmas lunch with all of them tomorrow."

His head came up, his eyes bright. "Really? That'll be a blast."

It would be, but she still had to tease him. She waited until his mouth was full of cornbread. "Because our Christmases are not?"

He sputtered, crumbs flying. "No. I love our Christmases. Even when we spend the day with your parents. Or your sister. But even those were... quiet, I guess."

She thought back to Christmas mornings with her sister, tossing wrapping paper everywhere while their parents looked on and laughed. She imagined Christmas morning would be complete chaos at Jeff's house this year, all those grandkids.

She wished she'd been able to give that to Alex.

She and Rob had made so many plans. Reaching for his hand, she gave him a soft smile. Not a sad one, just gentle, accepting, appreciating their life for the joy it had brought them both.

"You've never had a big rowdy Christmas."

"I'm not complaining," he said as she let him go. "Just saying with all those little kids, it'll be great. I mean, Santa Claus is for the kids, right?"

She pointed at him with her spoon. "And me. Don't forget me."

"How could I ever forget you? Or your obsession?"

"It's not an obsession," she said as Alex raised a brow. "It's... true love."

NINE

Maddie and Alex had been in Jeff's house more times than she could count, just like he'd been in hers. She knew the layout and decor as well as she knew her own. Most of it, anyway. She'd only been upstairs a few times when his girls were young and she, and an even younger Alex, had stood in for Jeff when he'd been called out to a fire.

It hadn't happened often but there had been a

few times when the fire had kept him and she'd ended up sleeping over, getting the girls dressed and ready for school the next morning before bringing them home with her and feeding them breakfast with Alex.

While they'd eaten, she'd grabbed everything she and Alex would need for the day and rushed through a three-minute shower. After delivering the girls to school and dropping Alex at daycare, she'd made her way to work. And collapsed.

When that had happened, Jeff had always stopped at the clinic to thank her, to ask how the girls had done overnight, to thank her again. Usually with doughnuts.

He could've texted. He never had.

Now, standing just inside his front door, she surveyed the scene in front of her. His tree stood in the corner of the great room, looking so festive with all the gifts still beneath it. Even more had been opened, the paper torn, the bows bedraggled.

She loved it.

Two of his grands, one of Ashley's girls and one of Audrey's boys, sat curled into opposite ends of the couch, candy canes hooked in their mouths, reading. The youngest boy wore a sweatshirt inside out with the tags at his throat choking him.

Jeff's sons-in-law sat in the middle of the floor with the rest of the bunch and some sort of Lego creature she was pretty sure the older boys could've built in half the time.

She laughed as Alex, who'd first taken a laundry basket loaded with food to the kitchen, reappeared and vaulted the couch and joined the construction crew.

The kids squealed, and the men called out greetings, thanking her for the cookies she'd sent over the day before. The kids followed suit, thanking her too. A classic Rudolph movie played muted in the background. The house smelled of roasting turkey and sweet potatoes and something sweet with cherries. A cobbler, maybe?

It was glorious, she thought with a rush of joy tumbling through her stomach, though she decided that was probably hunger.

And anticipation.

And Jeff.

She'd been looking forward to this day for so long. And now that it was here, she never wanted it to end. Emotion overwhelmed her. Seeing all of Jeff's grandkids with their dads and Alex crowded into the great room... It was perfect. Amazing.

It was Christmas.

And then Jeff appeared from the kitchen, an apron around his waist, a dish towel in his hands. He stopped and grinned when he saw her. He walked toward her, stopping when she held out a fresh-from-the-oven bread pan.

"Hot bananas. Just for you."

He took it, oven mitts and all, lifting the edge of the foil and breathing in, his eyes closed, his expression euphoric. Then he opened them and looked at her. He wrapped an arm around her neck and whispered in her ear.

"I'm glad you kept feeding me. Now let me get a fork."

Still feeling his scruff against her cheek, she followed him to the kitchen. There, both Audrey and Ashley jumped up and threw their arms wide.

"Merry Christmas!" they yelled in unison.

Maddie hugged them both, watching Jeff's eyes drift closed again as he forked a huge bite of banana bread into his mouth and groaned.

"You're going to spoil your lunch," she told him as the twins turned to see what all the noise was about.

"This is my lunch," he said after another bite. "My dinner. My dessert. Tomorrow's breakfast."

Ashley leaned over and grabbed the pan from

his hands. Then grabbed his fork. She took a bite, then handed the fork to her sister. "Maddie! This is amazing!"

"I'm going to need the recipe," Ashley said, resealing the foil and setting the pan on top of Jeff's fridge. He eyed it with calculated intent, but Ashley held up one index finger. "Don't even think about it."

"I will not stop thinking about it."

"Fine. You can think. You cannot touch."

"At least not until after the feasting is done." It was Audrey who gave her father a reprieve. Jeff hung his head and let out a sigh of faux defeat, lifting his hands in surrender. Maddie thought her heart might burst with all she was feeling.

Because at the moment, she had never loved him more.

Audrey turned toward her then, grabbing her hand and pressing it to her own heart. Her eyes swam with joyous emotion. "Maddie, thank you for all of this because I know Dad didn't do it on his own."

Jeff lifted one hand. "I hung her lights on my own."

"And they look fab," Ashley said. "But this much food, and everything in the freezer... It's a month's worth of work. How long did the lights take you?"

Jeff reached up to scratch the back of his neck. "It took me nearly a month to get around to it."

"Exactly," Ashley said, as both Audrey and Maddie tried not to laugh.

Maddie failed miserably, her cheeks aching as she finally pulled in a deep breath. Then she turned to Audrey. "You're welcome. Now what can I do?"

"You can call the others to the dining room," Ashley said, motioning her father forward to carry the turkey. "Everything's ready. Let's eat."

"I will never get used to Alex being all grown up," Audrey said.

"It's like we totally missed the years between middle school and college," Ashley added.

Maddie was in Jeff's kitchen with his girls, Audrey the blue-eyed blonde of her mother and Ashley the dark-haired image of Jeff. They were so much alike in so many ways, but both had told her repeatedly growing up they were glad they didn't look the same.

"It's just as hard for me to see the two of you as wives and mothers. It's like time has no meaning anymore. It just flies." *And suddenly you realize you're middle-aged.*

It was easier now to laugh about it. Though she wasn't sure she'd ever forgive Jeff. "Your father pointed that out to me recently. By telling me we were both middle-aged."

Ashley gasped, a wet fist going to her hip. "He did not."

Maddie nodded. "It's been the running joke this month. Even if it's not funny."

While Maddie scraped uneaten and unsalvage-able food from the last two kids' plates into the trash, Ashley turned off the water and reached for a towel to dry her hands.

Maddie handed her the plates, and she stacked them with the others, giving Maddie a look.

"What?" she asked when Audrey joined her sister, both of them smiling at her. "Do I have a cranberry salad mustache?"

Jeff's daughters looked at each other. Then Audrey opened the door to the walk-in pantry and came out with a gaily colored gift bag. She handed it to Maddie.

"What's going on?" Maddie asked, drying her hands before accepting the bag.

"It's Christmas," Audrey said. "Christmas means gifts."

Gifts made Maddie so nervous. She took it with shaking hands. "You invited us to your family gathering. That's gift enough."

"Oh, please," Ashley said, using her shoulder to push away a tendril of dark hair from her face. "You and Dad did most of the cooking, anyway. If he hadn't invited you, we would have. The cranberry salad was great."

"Great is easy with the recipe right in front of you," Maddie said, remembering Jeff Googling the one for her mother's banana cake. Remembering him peeling all those bananas. Remembering him telling her that he'd shared one with a three-year-old Alex.

Her son, who'd called him Daddy. She took a deep breath.

And she was just about to peer into the gift bag when Audrey said, "He's crazy about you, you know."

Maddie blinked and asked the obvious.

"Who?"

Ashley answered, dropping her voice to a whisper. "Daddy, of course."

"Yeah," Audrey said, crimping foil around the rest of the sweet potatoes. "He's been crazy about you forever."

Dizziness swept through Maddie, unbalancing her as she shook her head. "We're just friends. We've been friends forever. That's all it is."

"Nope," Ashley said, then Audrey expounded, "Yes. You've been friends forever. But that's not all it is. That hasn't been all it is for years."

Had Lisa been right? Had Maddie failed to pay attention? To see what was right under her nose? Had she been so focused on work and raising Alex that she'd missed what even his daughters had seen? "I'm sorry. I don't mean to doubt you—"

Audrey looked at Ashley, her blue-eyed gaze narrowed. "I think it started right about the time he was promoted. We were in high school. He finally had more time for himself."

Ashley shook her head, her novelty Christmas light earrings sparkling. "It was before that. Maybe the time you sprained your ankle in gymnastics."

"I remember that. He called me, frantic. He

had all the discharge instructions from the ER, but he still called me."

"Of course he called you," Ashley said with a laugh, turning to rinse the rest of the plates. "He never trusted us to anyone but you."

"Wait." Audrey held up one finger. She looked to Maddie. "It was before that. Remember that day he had you pick us up at school? When the power went out?"

Ashley cut off the water again and reached for a towel. "We were like in fifth grade, right? It was a car crash, a high-speed chase. The driver hit a pole and took off. Dad was on scene and wanted us out of there."

Audrey nodded as she refilled her glass with iced tea. "Yeah. You brought us back to the clinic with you. He was still pretty upset when he got there. When he hugged you."

"I remember." Maddie hadn't thought about that day in ages. Or that hug.

"It went on forever," Audrey said. "I think he might've been crying."

"He'd been worried," Maddie said, remembering the feel of Jeff's whole body shaking. And so very thankful Alex had been safely in daycare that day. "The parish sheriffs were all over the campus. They couldn't find the driver. It was chaos."

"I'm surprised you got through," Ashley said. Then Audrey added, "It was probably the scrubs. And that Dad knew most of the officers there."

Maddie had known a few of them, too. What she didn't know was how she'd gotten Jeff's girls safely away, but she'd been so relieved that she had.

"You gave Daddy the peace he needed to do his job. He didn't have to worry about us. You lifted that burden from him. You've done it for him over and over."

Ashley nodded in agreement. "In so many ways. Not just about us."

Maddie took a deep breath. She didn't know what to say.

Ashley went on, filling the silence. "One of you is going to have to cross the street and get this thing started."

Maddie laughed. Jeff's girls were so cute. "Is that all it takes? Crossing the street? Because we've been doing that for years, too."

Audrey poured the rest of the cranberry salad into a smaller bowl and handed the empty to Ashley. "And in all that time, how many men have you dated?"

"Well, none. I had Alex."

"Dad's never dated either. Not once."

"He had both of you to raise."

"And both of us have been gone for a lot of years. Still no dates."

Maddie hadn't ever really thought about that. Jeff dating. She didn't want to think about it now. "I guess the time just hasn't been right."

"Now it is," Ashley said. "As long as you're just as crazy about him."

Maddie's face heated. She was certain her cheeks were Santa Claus red. "I'm going to grab some dessert before my son goes back for thirds or fourths or whatever helping he's on now."

"And then you're going to go relax in the living room," Ashley said, loading the last of Jeff's everyday dishes into the dishwasher. "We'll be there in a minute."

"Wait," Audrey called, and Maddie turned. "First you have to open the gift!"

"I highly recommend the banana cake. The icing's like a brown sugar fudge."

"Is it now?" Smiling, Maddie stood in front of the small table in the dining room that held all the desserts. There were so many desserts and not a lot left of any.

Jeff's sons-in-law and Alex were probably responsible for the bulk of the destruction, but she'd seen the kids sneaking in with empty plates and out with uneven and ragged slices of the cakes and pies. She hadn't seen them up close to know.

What was left behind spoke clearly.

"Or..." Jeff pointed to the chocolate cake she'd made that Alex had nearly demolished on his own. "That chocolate one there with the white icing. It's in high demand. By a nineteen-year-old college kid who's a pretty good judge of these things."

"You don't say." Okay, she was being coy, which wasn't like her, but it was fun teasing wiht Jeff.

"He's a pretty smart kid. Smarter than us, I suspect."

Warmth bloomed near Maddie's heart. Her son was so predictable, and she adored that about him. He was back in the great room with the kids and their dads.

She could hear them talking. They were discussing aa popular video game. It was so nice, the easy conversations, casual, peaceful.

Ashley and Audrey were still dealing with the food storage. Laughing, they'd had to shoo away their husbands whose offers of help had meant filling their plate for the third time.

Maddie looked over at Jeff, filled with as much joy as she was food. "I'm not sure I need more sugar after that cranberry salad."

"Ahh, but isn't that what holidays are for? Overindulging in sweetness?" His gaze didn't leave her face and she had a feeling he wasn't talking about just desserts.

"It's all so delicious."

"Pretty amazing stuff, right?" He arched both brows. "Like those shortbread cookies. I think the girls ate a dozen each before you got here."

That made Maddie happy. "So you weren't the only one ruining your appetite."

"Like father, like daughters."

"A family tradition."

"It's funny what sticks with your kids," he said. "You never know what's going to impress them."

"Cookies are always a crowd pleaser."

"So are loving neighbors." He lower his voice, and leaned closer.

Her heart fluttered at his attention. He made her feel wanted—treasured.

"You mean a lot to my girls," he said.

"They mean a lot to me."

"I love this time of year," he said. "When people take stock of the best things in their lives."

"Did you see what your girls got me?" Maddie murmured.

She held out the snow globes the girls had wrapped in colored tissue paper and tucked into the gift bag. One was Santa, flat on his back, eyes closed, obviously snoring. The other was Rudolph in a mirror of his position.

"Cute," he said.

"I adore them and I'm not just talking about the snow globes."

He nodded, his hands shoved deep in his jeans pockets. He'd ditched his apron before dinner and wore a ridiculous Christmas sweater Audrey's kids had picked out for him.

Ashley's kids had given him an equally ridiculous Santa hat with long, blond hair. He was dutifully wearing that, too. He was a good sport and Maddie admired him for it.

"They love you like a mother, you know," Jeff said. "You're the closest thing they've ever had."

Tears rose to choke her. "Today has been wonderful. I'm so glad we did this."

"There wouldn't have been a today without you."

"All I did was—"

"Everything." His voice was low, gritty and raw. "You planned. You shopped. You cooked—"

She shook her head. "We both did all of those things."

He laughed, a soft self-deprecating sound. "You're being way too generous, Maddie."

"I am not." Oh, but she loved hearing him say her name. "You bought trees. You hung lights. Most importantly, you plugged in the lights."

He shrugged. "I *am* a trained professional."

"Thank you for making me laugh."

"I live to serve." He winked. Consider it my life's purpose to make you laugh." His widening smile teased.

"You do it all the time. You've always done it. You seem to know when I need it."

"Some of that's a defense mechanism," he said, his expression tender, his brown eyes sparkling.

"Huh?" She blinked. "How's that?"

"I hate seeing you cry."

She sniffed, breathing in all the sugary smells. "Happy tears are okay to cry."

"Not really," he said, and she laughed again.

Then she grimaced. "I'm sorry I didn't get you anything."

"Uh, excuse me? What about the incredible banana bread you made? Not to mention that chocolate cake I can't stop raving about. And the banana cake. And the most mouthwatering pot roast and potato soup ever. Need I go on?" said Jeff, pretending to scold her.

Maddie smirked, "You know very well what I mean. An actual wrapped present," she said.

"I would've made you take it back if you had. You don't need to spend your hard earned money on my crusty old hide."

She narrowed her gaze. "You don't even know what it was that I didn't give you."

"Doesn't matter what it wasn't. You've given me everything I'll ever need."

Is that what he thought? What he truly thought?

She loved him so much. And it wasn't just the season. She couldn't imagine life without him.

She couldn't imagine standing here another

moment and not throwing her arms around his neck and feeling his warmth and his strength and all the things he gave her.

And so she didn't. She took one step, then another.

And then he was there, and she held him and held him and whispered into his ear, "Thank you. This was the best Christmas ever."

"You're welcome. And thank you for the same." He squeezed her, but he didn't let her go. "None of this would've happened without you."

"Without you," she said.

And then he turned his head, his lips at her ear. "Without us."

TEN

"Just text Jeff already," Alex said, his deep teasing voice breaking into Maddie's thoughts.

She glanced over to where he was sprawled the length of the couch, a pillow and one arm beneath his head, his free hand—and his gaze —glued to his phone. He hadn't even looked at her when he spoke, just continued to scroll.

It was early Christmas evening, dark outside, a

fire burning in the fireplace, the lights on the tree twinkling and casting sparkling bursts of color to reflect off the hardwood floor's shine.

They'd spent much of the afternoon with the Murphy family, but then it had been time to come home, to leave Jeff and his bunch to enjoy the rest of their holiday without the intrusion of friends and neighbors.

Except Maddie had never felt as if she and Alex were intruding. And she'd definitely felt—for weeks now, in fact—like more than a friend or a neighbor. This afternoon had cemented that, his family, her family, one big happy family. And holding him.

Curled up in her cushy oversized chair, Maddie frowned and muted the TV, pausing the Christmas movie she wasn't really watching. Because Alex was right. She was thinking about Jeff, wondering about Jeff, wanting to talk to Jeff.

She couldn't get him out of her head, especially after watching him at lunch with his grandkids. During the meal, each of them, one at a time, had brought their plate to him for another helping of one thing or another.

They'd had to circle the table to reach his chair when they could have easily asked their parents

CHRISTMAS BEACH PROPOSAL 125

who were seated close. It had required a lot of passing dishes the length of the table, resulting in a lot of heartwarming laughter.

The kids had got a huge kick out of the game, a couple of them coming back more than once. And Jeff had loved every minute. The grin on his face never faded and Maddie's love for him had made it near impossible to focus on the company or the food the two of them had spent so much time preparing.

Every dish made her think of Jeff chopping or grating or stirring while she found the right dishes and wrap for the freezer, the right measuring cups and spoons.

They'd talked endlessly and downed way too much coffee and too many cookies. She hadn't thought twice about the calories or the caffeine. Instead, she'd wondered what it would be like for that to be her life, for Jeff to be her life.

Today had been the best Christmas Day she'd had in ages.

When Alex was young, they'd spent many of the holidays with her sister's family. Other times, all of them had joined her parents to celebrate the day. As Alex had gotten older and needed to be home for school events or for work, she'd made the holiday special for the two of them, their own little family.

But today—

"Mom."

She gave him her attention and played dumb. "What?"

He was still scrolling, his focus divided between written and verbal conversation like most everyone his age. "Jeff. Text him. See what he's up to."

It would be so easy to do. Tell him she didn't want to interrupt his family time, but she was here if he wanted to chat, to come over. Her skin heated as her pulse raced beneath it. Easy, sure, but a very bad idea. They'd have time later. Neither of them was going anywhere. "He's got six grandkids visiting. I know exactly what he's up to."

"Could be he needs a grandkid break. Could be he's also not watching a Christmas movie and wondering if he should text you."

Her pulse raced faster at the thought. Her skin grew flushed. "We don't all live on our phones, you know."

"Phone, tablet, laptop, game console, TV. They're all still screens."

Smarty-pants. "This is our holiday, Alex. I will not ruin our tradition."

He arched a brow. "You're barely here, Mom. Even less so than usual."

This time, she clicked off the television and set the remote on the lamp table. This was important. "What do you mean?"

Alex swiped his phone dark and swung his feet to the floor. He held the device between both hands, his elbows on his knees. It took him a moment to find what he wanted to say, leaving Maddie's stomach to tangle and knot while she waited.

Had she failed him somehow? Somewhere? She knew she had. She could name and number the ways. But not here. Not now. She had always put him first, given him all of her attention, every bit of her time, whatever he needed... Hadn't she?

This was something more than that. And she feared it was about her.

When he finally figured it all out and looked at her, his expression mirrored every bit of the love for him that left her breathless. His eyes were solemn when he smiled and even that was tremulous, as if he didn't want to hurt her feelings, as if even that couldn't keep him from getting whatever this was off his chest.

He took a deep breath while Maddie held hers.

"You've been in love with Jeff Murphy since my freshman year. Maybe even longer. But I probably wasn't old enough to notice until that night he had to come pick me up from football practice. Do you remember?" he asked.

She nodded because she would never forget.

"You couldn't get to the school because of the rain. I think you had a flat," he said.

"I did have a flat," she said, the fear of that moment skittering down her spine. She'd flown out the clinic's rear exit, slipping to a stop and getting drenched to her skin as she stared at her SUV sitting lopsided in its spot.

"Jeff heard about the lightning strike at the field house. Or maybe it was just that he was at the firehouse when Coach called 9-1-1. Anyhow, when he got there, the first thing he did was order me to his truck to wait. I guess he meant for you."

Maddie shook her head. "I'd texted him. Told him I was stuck at the clinic." The wait for his return text had been interminable. The wait to get her tire changed and make the drive home even more so. And still she'd beat them there.

"Right. Anyhow, he wasn't on duty, but he stayed long enough to make sure the fire was under control. And then when we got home..."

Maddie closed her eyes, tears welling as she remembered that day, her smile and her voice both shaky. It didn't matter that Jeff had texted to let her know he had Alex and her son was safe. "I didn't think you'd ever get here."

"And when I did"—Alex shifted around to face her, cocking a knee onto the couch, cocking his head, giving her a cocky grin—"when *we* did, you wrapped me up in one arm but wrapped the rest of yourself up in Jeff."

Maddie's face heated, her cheeks burned, her nape felt blistered. "I was relieved. Waiting is the worst when what you're waiting for is to see for yourself that your child isn't hurt."

"Uh-huh," Alex said with a grin. "That's why you didn't even stop me from pulling away or watch me run upstairs to shower. You just stood there hugging Jeff."

Guilty as charged. "That doesn't mean I'm in love with him."

"But you are," Alex said, a too-knowing brow lifting... knowingly.

"I love him, yes," she said, hoping her confession came off with some believability. "Just like I love Audrey and Ashley. We're friends. We're neighbors. But that's all."

The expression on Alex's face was way too grown up. When had he become so grown up? "You're wasting time."

She frowned. "What?"

"Neither one of you is getting any younger."

"Alexander Robert!" She threw the remote at him.

He caught it like the wide receiver he'd been all four years of high school. "Just tellin' it like it is."

"I'll show you *like it is*," she said as he pushed to his feet and advanced.

"Give me your phone." He said it at the same time he swooped in and grabbed it off her lamp table, leaving the remote in its place.

"Alex!" She jumped up, but he was six inches taller than her, many pounds heavier than her, twenty-nine years younger than her, and too strong for her to manhandle.

"There," he said, handing it back, damage done.

She glared at him, anticipation like snowflakes on her skin. She didn't yet look at what he'd texted to Jeff. She didn't want to know even more than she did.

But she did want to know if Jeff would

respond. What he was thinking. How long it would take. "You are grounded."

"I'll take it," he said with a laugh.

She glared back. "Forever."

And then his expression softened, his smile, his eyes. "As long as you're happy."

That stopped her. "Really?

He nodded, perching on the edge of the couch cushion nearest to her chair. "Jeff makes you happy, Mom. I know I'm a kid, even if I'm an adult one, but I'm your kid and you are never happier than when Jeff's around."

"I'm happiest when you're around."

"I know," he said, and she thought he was placating her. As if he didn't doubt her love for him but knew her feelings for Jeff were equally strong. Just a... different strong.

She was on the verge of some very loud and snotty tears but was stopped when her phone dinged. She left it on the table, her gaze held by her son's. When had he become so observant? So kind? So empathetic?

Had she actually done this? Raised that tiny squirming baby to be this amazing young man? To be the epitome of the father he'd never known, even while he looked exactly like her?

The tears she'd been holding at bay spilled before she could turn. Alex reached for her, pulled her close, and hugged her like she needed to be hugged, in the best way possible, with so much love and tenderness and compassion.

"I love you, Mom. Now check your texts."

Before she could, a knock sounded on the front door. Her stomach tumbled and landed on her feet. "What did you say to him?"

Alex shrugged and turned for the door. "Just asked him if he was ready for quieter company."

Heat flooded her face. She pointed sternly at her son. "You tell him that was you."

He saluted her, swung open the door, and before Jeff could speak, said, "I sent the text. Not Mom."

Jeff stopped with one foot on the threshold, looking from Alex to Maddie. "Oh."

Maddie hung her head and shook it. "I am so sorry. This is your family time. And feel free to add Alex to your brood since once he's done with his time-out, he'll be up for adoption."

Jeff snorted and looked at Alex. "They're doing a Marvel Universe movie marathon."

"Sweet," Alex said, grabbing his hoodie from the coatrack next to the door.

"And they've got fudge, cookies, and two whole pecan pies."

"Make that one whole pecan pie," he said, adding, "see ya, Mom," then closing the front door behind him after Jeff had stepped inside.

He shoved his hands deep in his pockets and stayed where he was. "You said you were lonely."

Her head came up. "When?"

He held up his phone. "On your text. You asked if I wanted some quieter company and said you were lonely."

Embarrassment wasn't a big enough word to describe the hot prickles covering her skin. "He's disowned."

Jeff returned his phone to his pocket and came farther into the room. "He's a good kid."

"I know."

"Wanna know something else?"

"Sure."

"I actually am kinda lonely. I mean, there are ten people, now eleven, sprawled around in my den stuffing their faces. I shouldn't be." He held her gaze. "But I am."

"You can be surrounded by multitudes and still be lonely," she said, motioning him toward the kitchen.

"Yeah," he said and followed her.

"Want some coffee?" Was it too late for coffee? "Tea? Coke?" Great. More caffeine options. "Water?"

"Coffee would be great," he said and kept following. "Is it weird that I was never lonely when raising the girls on my own?"

"Not really. It was a different time of your life. You had to be there for them, focused on them." She grabbed two mugs from the cupboard and added a clean filter to the coffeemaker, scooping in coffee and pouring in water. "You didn't have time to be lonely. Or much time for yourself."

He'd leaned an elbow on the counter and was studying her as she worked even though he'd seen her make coffee dozens, hundreds of times. "Were you lonely? When it was just you and Alex? I mean, it's still just you and Alex..."

She nodded. She knew what he meant. "Yeah, but our situations weren't the same. Rob was here for breakfast and gone by suppertime."

"I'm so sorry that happened to you."

"Thank you." She turned to lean back against the counter, wondering why in the world this was where their conversation had gone. On Christmas, of all days. "It was nearly half my lifetime ago. But that doesn't keep me from wondering who I'd be now if it hadn't. If Rob and I had raised Alex together. Had a life together."

"I get that," he said, then went quiet as the coffee reached the end of its brewing cycle and began to sputter and steam. "Alex is a great kid. A great man. Rob would be proud."

"I think so too. I mean, it takes a village, but in the end our kids are our kids." She fetched half-and-half from the fridge and set it on the table. Jeff filled their mugs while she found spoons and sweetener and a tin of shortbread cookies. "I'm pretty proud of him myself. And I know you're proud of the girls."

"Every single day," he said as they sat, the room still and smelling of sweet cookies and coffee. Maddie filled her lungs and accepted the peace that enveloped her.

She was warm. She was comfortable. She wasn't the least bit lonely anymore.

And she was head over heels in love. It was time to tell him.

Once she figured out how.

"Of course, your being a grandfather really does make you older than me," she said, and he snorted coffee.

"Thanks," he said, reaching for the paper towel she handed him. "And I'm older than you because I was born the year before. Nothing to do with having six grandkids... Six. Wow." He shook his head. "At least that gives me a reason to feel older than I am."

Maddie laughed. "Most of the time I don't feel any older than I did when Alex was born. And then I'll sneeze and break a rib. Or cough and throw out my back."

"I hear you," he said, picking up a cookie and dunking it in his coffee. "I'm counting the days to retirement."

This time, she was the one to sputter. "Now that sounds like an old man talking."

He smiled at that as he leaned to the side to fish something out of his pocket. He handed her a small box wrapped similarly to the ones his daughters had given her earlier today. "Here."

"You people and your snow globes," she said, though this one felt much lighter.

"Open it." It was his only response.

Since those from his daughters, and the one from Alex, had been so late in coming, she thought she might leave them all on the mantel until next year. "On it, boss."

"No need to call me boss," he said, watching as she folded back the flaps.

Behind her, the refrigerator kicked on, buzzing. From the living room, bells on the tree jingled as the heater blew warm air. The house creaked with the changes in temperature, with the slight movement every time she breathed.

Oh, what was happening here?

Inside, instead of a snow globe, was a jeweler's ring box. She lifted it out, setting the gift packaging on the kitchen table. Then she held it, one hand on the bottom, one on the hinged top, staring at Jeff as emotion flooded her.

"What do you want me to call you?"

ELEVEN

Maddie couldn't breathe, so she couldn't hold her breath while she waited for Jeff's answer. She couldn't think. She couldn't feel her fingers or her toes.

She couldn't smell the coffee or the cookies or hear any of the noises in the house.

All she heard was the roaring in her ears. The room seemed to tilt. Or maybe it was her entire world that was headed for the unknown of the upside down.

All she knew was Jeff.

He was the only reason she hadn't fallen out of her seat and crashed to the floor.

"I was thinking husband would be nice." He shrugged, his expression belying the dismissive motion. It was strained, as if his nerves had pulled tight.

That was pretty easy to understand since she thought if she moved she might snap. But the rest of his expression... He was happy. So very happy.

Was it the season? Was it having his family close?

Was it his anticipation of her response?

Her own nerves popped and sizzled.

Jeff went on. "And whatever term of endearment you're comfortable with. Unless you'd rather just call me Jeff."

"Jeff."

"That works," he said a little bit sheepishly.

"I don't mean... That's not what I mean... I mean... Oh, Jeff." Her thoughts were a jumbled mess. She couldn't make sense of anything to say. The constriction in her chest felt like a blood pressure cuff about to explode.

Her voice came out strangled. "What is this?"

"A proposal? Which I'm mangling."

"A proposal."

He nodded and laced his hands together on top of the table. "Yep."

"You want to marry me?" Her pulse thundered in her ears. Had she heard him right? Had he heard her? She didn't even know if her voice had registered.

"I do. Or should I save that for the ceremony?"

"But... why?"

The look he gave her then said the reason should be obvious. His smile was beatific, as if he couldn't possibly be happier than he was in this moment.

As if he'd never been this happy in his life. "Because I love you."

"Oh." More thunder in ears. Lightning. Rain... though that was probably the tears running down her cheeks. He loved her. Jeff Murphy loved her.

If Jeff Murphy loved her, why was she crying?

"I think I've loved you since you asked me to come over and help you convert Alex's crib into a toddler bed. But it was too soon. After Rob," he said and frowned down at his hands now splayed on the table. "And then there were my girls and work and your job and... Life just went on, you over here, me across the street, both of us coming and going on Brown Bark Lane."

"That was very poetic." Her comment didn't exactly lighten the mood, but it was a space they both needed. A breather. A bit of their old selves in the face of this new world. The gift of this new world.

A world where Jeff Murphy loved her.

"I aim to please," he said.

And for a long moment, that was all. She stared at the box. He stared at his coffee. The room seethed with tension and questions and the scent of pine filtered its way through all of that to remind her of the season. The joy. The celebration.

Families and friends and a respite from the day-to-day, where homes burned to the ground and the smallest of children suffered. They'd both chosen careers that would put them in those crosshairs, seeing the need, seeing the loss.

Seeing the love as helping hands reached down.

And yet it had taken until now for their time to be right. They'd both had to get through what life had served up when they were young and learning to navigate those dark days. Days that molded them, years that seasoned them.

Finally, she had to ask, "And you've loved me all this time?"

He nodded. Then, before she could say more, he started again, frowning, focused. "Something happened after the fire last year. Something that changed things."

"How so?" Her question came out as a whisper, waiting.

He shoved out a stream of breath. "I saw you standing there holding on to Alex and it hit me I could lose you. If things had gone differently that night, I might've been standing there looking at nothing but ashes. I almost told you then how I felt, but I was wiped out and I knew you didn't have the room for more."

She got it. She'd looked at what had burned and held Alex so tight he'd laughed and told her over and over he was fine, he wasn't going anywhere; they were both good.

"I'd really like you to open the box."

"I'm afraid to," she said, lifting her gaze to meet his.

"Why?" he asked, wrapping his hands so tightly around his mug she feared the ceramic would shatter. "What in the world do you have to be afraid of? Because I know it's not me."

"It's not you. It could never be you. It's—"

"Don't say it's me. Like you me. Not me."

She wanted to laugh. He always made her want to laugh. She loved that about him. She loved so many things about him. But... "It *is* me. Sort of. I don't want to mess things up. Our friendship. You and me. Because if this box holds what I think it does..." She was rambling and she was going to ruin everything. She gave a quick shake of her head and tried again. "Starting over would make everything... new, different."

"New and different is okay. Starting over is okay."

"Do you know how many times I've had to start over?"

"Probably as many as I have," he said, taking the wind from her sails.

"I'm sorry. I know you have." What was wrong with her? She rubbed at the ache in her forehead. "I don't know what's wrong with me."

"It's the last week of the year." He reached over and covered her free hand, scooting the ring box to the side. "Post-Christmas exhaustion. Alex will leave again soon."

"And I'll be alone again soon. Starting over." Feeling sorry for herself. Being pathetic.

She stood and carried her mug to the sink, staring out the window into the dark but seeing her reflection in the glass. She wanted this; she wanted *him*, but she was so afraid taking things with Jeff further would leave her without this Jeff whom she loved so very much. What in the world was wrong with her? Just because she'd lost Rob...

Snap out of it, Madelyn. You're about to mess up the best thing that's happened to you since Alex was born. You will not lose Jeff.

Jeff's chair legs scraped the floor as he pushed back from the table. She felt his intent, his sincerity, his dependable solidity as he moved toward her, his steps slow, his steps sure. His steps bringing him to where she stood before she was ready.

"No. Not this time. I'll be here."

"I know."

"Do you?"

"Of course. You've always been here."

"Didn't think you'd noticed."

"Why would you say that? I wouldn't have survived last year's fire without you. Or Alex's first year of high school football and that lightning strike. Or his driver's ed. You were there when I couldn't be. When he had no one else."

"A father."

That wasn't what she meant. She was handling this so poorly. "You're his friend. And you made it easier for him. In every way."

"I love Alex like he's my own, but I know he's not. And everything I've ever done for him has been to fill that gap in his life. But I also did it for you."

"And I appreciate that—"

"No, Maddie. Not for you as his mother. Not to give him what you couldn't, what Rob would have if he'd been here. I did it for you. Because of how I feel about you. Because of wanting to make things easier on you."

"Jeff—"

"Let me finish while I can, or I never will." Arms crossed, he leaned against the counter beside her and stared down at his feet clad in a brand-new pair of boots. He smelled like coffee and cookies and pine and soap and mostly like Jeff. All of him so very familiar. So very... hers. "I don't know why it happened this year, unless last year's to blame, but it's like Santa threw a switch and my entire life lit up that day I ran into you in Penny's."

She smiled at the memory, knowing that day had sent her own avalanche of emotions tumbling.

"We were both so lost. Not knowing what we were doing. Overwhelmed. Stressed."

"And look where we are now. There is no stress. There is no whelm."

She snorted. "I don't think you can use that as a noun."

"Sure I can. And if you don't open that box," he said, nodding toward the table, "I'm going to be right back there, lost, stressed, super whelmed."

She smiled. She loved this man. What would she have done if he hadn't been part of her life? Why was she hesitating? What hadn't she opened the box?

She dropped her gaze and took a deep breath and let her skin absorb every bit of the joy swirling through the room. Then she picked up the box and lifted the lid. Pressing her fingers to her mouth, she stumbled back and collapsed to sit on the floor.

The ring was a twist of silver and gold, a conversation they'd once had, and he'd remembered. She loved silver, and he was a gold guy. And beautifully set into the design were two birthday gemstones, his diamond, her topaz, and a larger ruby in the center.

She looked up at him as he lowered himself to

sit beside her. "This is beautiful, Jeff. I've never seen anything this gorgeous."

"Good. Glad you think so."

"Ask me." She looked up at him, seeing every scar and wrinkle and mark of the life he'd lived. "Ask me again. Ask me right."

He took the box from her hand. Took the ring from the box. "Maddie Craig, I love you with every—

"Oh, Jeff. I love you so much. Alex told me earlier he'd known it since the field house fire. But I've known it for... It seems like forever."

"Sounds like we've wasted a lot of time."

"Nope." She shook her head. "We waited until the time was right."

"Is that a yes?"

"Yes, yes, yes, yes yes!" She leaned her head on his shoulder, listening to his sigh of relief billow out.

"Good to hear."

She giggled like she was twenty and not... not twenty. "Were you worried?"

"Not really. Or maybe a lot. Like a lot."

"What's the ruby for?" she asked because that was the only part she couldn't figure out. It wasn't Alex's birthstone, or Audrey and Ashley's. She didn't think it was related to his grandkids, his parents, or anyone in their family. The two of them didn't share any special anniversaries or memorable events.

Their lives as friends and neighbors had been beautifully simple. She was at a loss.

He shook his head. "Smart woman like you? I thought you'd figure that out first thing."

"Maybe I'm not as smart as you think," she said, pouting.

"Oh, you are," he said, scooting up beside her and wrapping his arm around her. "You just agreed to be my wife. That proves it."

It was the first time he'd touched her out of affection. She said, "You will not take back the proposal, will you?"

"As if," he said.

"Then what?"

"Santa, of course," he told her, dropping a soft kiss to her temple. Then another to the edge of her brow. "And Christmas. The most wonderful time of the year."

EPILOGUE

Christmas

Beach

One Year Later...

Maddie stood at the window of the master bedroom, gazing out at the backyard of her and Jeff's home on Brown Bark Lane. Even though it was the tail end of December, not a flake of snow dusted the winter-browned grass. The cloudless cerulean sky and bright sunlight belied the brisk chill in the air.

She smiled, thinking of how much her life had

changed in the past year. After Jeff had proposed on Christmas night, they'd decided not to have a long engagement.

Neither wanted to wait to start their new life together. They were married six months later, on a beautiful June day right here in their backyard.

Now here they were, Christmas morning once again. Their first as husband and wife. Maddie cherished these quiet moments before the organized chaos of Christmas Day commenced.

Soon their home would be filled with the sounds of Jeff making coffee, Alex thundering down the stairs, and later, the boisterous voices of Jeff's grandchildren.

This year, Audrey and her family would arrive first, early that afternoon. Ashley and her brood would get here later tonight. Maddie was grateful Jeff's girls and their families had chosen to spend Christmas together again.

She loved seeing Jeff interact with his daughters and playing with the grandkids. He was such a wonderful father and grandfather.

As Maddie turned from the window, her gaze fell on a framed photograph on the dresser. It had been taken on their wedding day. Jeff stood behind her, arms encircling her waist. Her hands covered his. They were both grinning from ear to ear. Joy and love shone from their faces.

Maddie picked up the frame, tracing her fingertips over Jeff's image. "Good morning, husband," she whispered.

"And a very merry Christmas morning to you, wife."

Jeff's voice made Maddie jump. She whirled around to find him leaning against the doorjamb, mussed hair and scruffy face making him look adorable. He wore red plaid flannel pajama bottoms and a long-sleeved black thermal shirt.

With a laugh, Maddie set the photo back on the dresser. "I didn't hear you come upstairs."

"I'm stealthy like a ninja." Jeff pushed off from the door and came toward her.

"Oh, is that what it is?" she teased. When he reached for her, she went willingly into his embrace. His arms closed around her, enveloping her in his warmth and familiar scent.

Jeff nuzzled his scruffy cheek against hers. "What were you doing up here all by yourself?"

"Just thinking." Maddie slid her arms around his waist and hugged him close.

"About?"

She tipped her head back to look up at him.

"How different this Christmas is. Our first as a married couple."

Jeff's lips curved. "I like the sound of that. Our first Christmas together." His smile faded. "I probably should've thought to get you a special present to commemorate it."

Maddie shook her head. "You've already given me the best gift—becoming my husband."

"You're gonna make me cry on Christmas morning, woman." Jeff kissed her forehead. "And we can't have that. I have a reputation to maintain."

"Oh, please." Maddie poked him in the stomach. "Alex and I both know you're a big softie."

Jeff captured her hand and brought it to his lips for a kiss. Then he tucked her against his side and headed for the stairs. "Speaking of Alex, is he still sleeping?"

Maddie nodded, slipping her arm around Jeff's waist. She loved that their new house had a main floor master suite. Alex occupied the upstairs bedroom since he was only home on school breaks. "I haven't heard a peep from him this morning. You know teenagers. He was probably up texting half the night."

At the bottom of the stairs, Jeff stopped and

glanced upward. "Think I should go jump on his bed like I do the grandkids on Christmas morning?"

The mental image made Maddie laugh out loud. "He'd probably punch you."

"You're probably right. "Jeff's eyes danced with humor. "But it sure would be fun."

In the kitchen, Jeff poured them each a mug of coffee while Maddie put a breakfast casserole into the oven. They carried their mugs to the living room, arranging themselves on the sofa facing the twinkling Christmas tree.

Maddie tucked her feet beneath her and leaned into Jeff's side. His arm came around her shoulders, holding her close. They sipped their coffees in contented silence, cozy in front of the fireplace Jeff had lit earlier.

"I can't believe it's been a year since you proposed," Maddie marveled. She angled her head to look up at him. "You remember how freaked out I got?"

Jeff chuckled. "I'll never forget it. You had me sweating bullets."

"I'm sorry about that. I just..." Maddie shook her head. "My emotions were all over the place.

First I was ecstatic because I was so in love with you. Then I panicked."

"Why?" Jeff asked curiously.

Maddie took a sip of coffee, gathering her thoughts. "I was afraid if we crossed the line from friends to more, I might lose what we had. And if that happened, I'd lose my best friend."

Jeff pressed a kiss to her temple. "You could never lose me. I loved you too much to let you go."

"I see that now," Maddie said softly. "But at the time, I was terrified of rocking the boat. Of changing everything between us."

"Yeah, but change can be good." Jeff gave her shoulders a little squeeze. "Just look at us now."

Maddie smiled up at him. "You're right. This change has been wonderful."

They kissed softly, then Jeff asked, "Be honest. Did you have any idea how I felt about you before I proposed?"

With a groan, Maddie dropped her head against his shoulder. "No! I was completely oblivious." She lifted her head. "Were you? Before that night, I mean. Did you know how I felt about you?"

Jeff was silent, a slight frown furrowing his brow. "I hoped you cared about me as more than a friend and neighbor. But I tried not to think about it too much." His lips twisted ruefully. "I didn't want to ruin our friendship if you didn't feel the same."

"We were both idiots, weren't we?" Maddie murmured.

"Colossal idiots," Jeff agreed, his eyes alight with humor.

Maddie curled into his side again with a contented sigh. "The important thing is, we finally got it right."

"Yes, we did." Jeff kissed the top of her head. "And I've never been happier."

They finished their coffee just as the oven timer dinged. While Jeff refilled their mugs, Maddie pulled the bubbly, cheesy casserole from the oven.

As if on cue, they heard the thud of feet hitting the floor upstairs. Maddie grinned. "I think the smell of food roused the beast from his slumber."

Jeff laughed. "That boy does love to eat."

A few minutes later, Alex shambled into the kitchen looking half-asleep. His dark hair stuck up in tufts all over his head. He wore flannel pajama bottoms and a long-sleeved thermal shirt just like Jeff's, making Maddie wonder if they'd secretly coordinated their loungewear.

"Merry Christmas, "she greeted him, pressing a mug of coffee into his hands.

Alex gulped down a few swallows, then mumbled something vaguely resembling "Merry Christmas" in return. Maddie and Jeff exchanged amused smiles over his head.

The three of them sat down to eat and Alex finally seemed to revive after consuming most of the casserole by himself. Maddie didn't mind. She was happy to see her son eating well after months of dubious dorm food.

"So, what time is everyone getting here?" Alex asked around a mouthful of food.

Maddie tore her gaze away from his bad table manners to answer. "Audrey and family should be here early afternoon. Ashley said they'd get here around dinnertime."

Alex nodded and shoveled in another bite. Maddie decided to stop watching him eat before she completely lost her appetite.

"We'll need to straighten up the house before they arrive," she mused. "And put the gifts under the tree."

"Yes, dear," Jeff said.

Alex snorted. Maddie chose to ignore both of them.

After breakfast, Maddie put Alex on vacuuming duty while she and Jeff tackled dusting and picking up stray items. In no time, the house was tidy. Jeff arranged the multitude of colorfully wrapped gifts beneath the tree while Maddie put the finishing touches on the Christmas Eve dinner she'd be serving that night.

Controller in hand, Alex seamlessly switched to his latest video game obsession, Fortnite, now that taking out the trash was done.

Maddie didn't mind his rapid escape. Better the virtual world than having him moping around, bored without school or friends around over winter break.

She knew once Jeff's grandkids arrived, he'd be back in the real world, ready to entertain them with made-up games, magic tricks, and funny voices. He never could resist being the fun cousin.

By midafternoon, Audrey and her family had arrived. Maddie enjoyed having Audrey's three children under her roof again. The girls, Emma and Ava, were twelve and ten. Their younger brother Luke was seven. He immediately gravitated to Alex, who had a wealth of video games and sporting knowledge to share with the boy.

Ashley's three kids were a bit younger—two

twin girls, Chloe and Zoe, age eight, and a rambunctious five-year-old son, Tyler. Maddie loved seeing Jeff light up whenever his grandchildren were around. She hoped they'd be blessed with a few more someday.

Later that evening, after a noisy, laughter-filled dinner around the dining room table, the family gathered in the living room to watch a Christmas movie. The little ones started out excitedly chattering away before eventually dropping off to sleep one by one.

Jeff sat in the corner of the sectional sofa with Maddie tucked against his side. His arm was draped loosely around her shoulders. Across from them, Ashley sat curled up with Audrey on the smaller love seat. Their husbands occupied the other couch with Alex sprawled across the ottoman.

Maddie sighed contentedly, letting her head rest against Jeff's broad shoulder. "This is perfect," she whispered. "I'm so happy."

Jeff turned his head to smile down at her. "Me too, sweetheart."

Onscreen, the movie characters celebrated Christmas in their quaint village. But Maddie was only vaguely aware of the story. Her focus stayed on the family surrounding her—especially the man by her side.

Jeff caught her gaze, eyebrows lifting in a silent question. Maddie just smiled and snuggled closer. She didn't have the words to explain how full her heart felt. How this Christmas was even more magical than the last because now she and Jeff were building a life together. But Jeff seemed to understand anyway.

His arm tightened around her in a brief hug. Then he dropped a kiss to her temple and turned back to the movie. As if he sensed Maddie's eyes still lingering on him, the corner of his mouth tipped up. Then he leaned over and whispered for only her to hear, "Just wait until I get you alone under the mistletoe later."

Maddie's cheeks heated, but she smiled. Oh, yes. She was looking forward to that, too. For now, she rested her head on Jeff's shoulder again and let herself be lulled by the sound of his steady heartbeat.

Christmas morning dawned bright and clear. Maddie woke slowly, smiling when she became aware of Jeff's arm banded securely around her waist beneath the covers. She snuggled back into his warmth with a contented sigh.

Jeff made a low, gravelly sound of approval. His arm tightened and he nuzzled her neck. "Morning."

Maddie laced her fingers through his. "Merry Christmas."

"Mmm... too early," Jeff complained sleepily. "Go back to sleep."

With a soft laugh, Maddie craned her neck to try and see his face. "I think it's after seven. We should probably get up soon before the horde descends."

Jeff groaned. "Oh, right. The chaos and mess are all part of the experience."

Maddie rolled over to face him. Jeff grudgingly lifted his head from the pillow to peer at her with one blurry eye. She smiled and smoothed his rumpled hair away from his forehead.

"Just think of the look on the kids' faces when they see everything Santa brought."

Jeff grunted, unimpressed by her sentimentality. He flopped onto his back with a huff. "Yeah, yeah. I'll have my cup of cheer once I have some actual coffee."

With another laugh, Maddie threw back the covers. Jeff made a half-hearted attempt to grab her back, but she evaded him easily. "Come on, Scrooge. Time to celebrate Christmas!"

Jeff eyed her over the top of the sheet he'd pulled up to his chin. "I liked it better when we were the only ones here to celebrate."

Warmth spread through Maddie's chest at his words. She knew Jeff loved his family, but it pleased her to hear he treasured their first Christmas in their new home as much as she did.

Perching on the edge of the bed, she rubbed his chest briskly. "Tell you what—after the chaos dies down tonight, we'll exchange gifts up here. Just the two of us. How does that sound?"

One corner of Jeff's mouth quirked upward. "It's a Christmas miracle. My wife knows exactly how to motivate me."

Maddie grinned and smacked him with a pillow. "Get your motivated self out of bed and start the coffee, please."

With a chuckle, Jeff sat up and pulled her close for a quick kiss. "Yes, dear."

Maddie couldn't help snuggling into him for a moment, arms winding around his neck. Jeff's hands slid beneath her sleep shirt. His palms were warm against her bare skin. When he deepened the kiss, Maddie momentarily forgot why they needed to get out of bed.

Then a loud thump sounded from upstairs, followed by the thunder of approaching footsteps. Jeff and Maddie broke apart with matching rueful smiles.

"And so it begins," Jeff pronounced.

Maddie patted his scruffy cheek consolingly. "At least we'll get to do this all over again when they leave."

Jeff stole another swift kiss. "Good point." He gave her a playful swat on the behind. "Now go get pretty. I'll start the coffee."

Still grinning, Maddie went to take a quick shower. By the time she made it downstairs, kids were already tearing into gifts with gusto. The living room floor was strewn with ribbons, bows, and discarded wrapping paper.

Jeff stood in the kitchen doorway cradling a large mug, surveying the madness with one eyebrow raised. He'd pulled on a pair of gray sleep pants and a long-sleeved Henley, feet bare. Maddie almost laughed at his disheveled, sleepy-eyed appearance combined with the "Bah Humbug" expression on his face.

Going up on tiptoe, she kissed his scruffy cheek. "Merry Christmas, my love."

Jeff's features softened. He wrapped one arm around her waist and kissed her temple. "Merry Christmas, Maddie." Against her hair, he murmured, "My gift to myself was marrying you this year."

Maddie's throat grew thick, a swell of emotion rising inside her. Without a word, she leaned into Jeff's side, hoping the simple press of closeness would convey what she couldn't yet say out loud— that being his wife was the only gift she needed this Christmas.

Their tender moment was interrupted by shouts of "Grandpa! Come see!" Jeff rolled his eyes, but obediently allowed himself to be towed over to the Christmas tree. Maddie watched him settle onto the floor amidst the sea of new toys, smile lines crinkling at the corners of his eyes. Her heart overflowed with love.

By the time all packages had been opened, the kids were hungry and wired on sugar. Maddie enlisted Alex and her sons-in-law to help wrangle everyone to the table for breakfast. Once fortified with French toast, bacon, and fruit, some of the initial excitement had worn off. The younger kids took their new toys off to play while the adults cleaned up.

Afterward, Audrey and Ashley's families left to spend a couple hours visiting their in-laws. The house seemed oddly quiet with just Maddie, Jeff, and Alex rattling around inside it. They passed the time playing board games until the others returned midafternoon.

Following a simple dinner of baked potato soup, salad, and bread, Maddie served the decadent chocolate cake she'd made yesterday. While Jeff helped with cleanup, Maddie packaged up leftovers for Audrey and Ashley's families to take with them.

Goodbyes were said amidst hugs all around. Maddie's eyes misted a bit as she watched them drive away. The house would feel empty again without those sweet, exuberant voices filling it up. But she consoled herself knowing they'd all be together again soon.

Inside, Jeff flopped onto the couch with a groan. "I'm exhausted. Remind me again why I thought it was a great idea to have everyone here?"

Alex dropped onto the opposite couch. "Because you love us?"

"Debatable," Jeff grunted. But the twinkle in his eyes gave him away.

Maddie perched on the sofa arm beside him. "Just think how quiet the house will seem now."

"Time for bed, my love," he said.

Maddie's pulse leaped as she stood and held out her hand.

Jeff entwined their fingers, his eyes filled with desire for her. She tugged him off the couch and led the way upstairs, anticipation singing through her veins.

This Christmas with Jeff had been utter chaos, yet completely magical. As he kicked their bedroom door shut and backed her toward the bed, Maddie knew the real enchantment was only just beginning.

Their love had withstood years as friends and neighbors. Now as husband and wife, it would blaze ever brighter. She couldn't wait to celebrate many more Christmases by Jeff's side.

But first, they had their own private party to enjoy. With a throaty laugh, Maddie tumbled onto the mattress, taking Jeff down with her.

★★*★*★*★*★*★

Dear Reader,

Cassidy and I are so deeply grateful that you've chosen to read our Christmas novella, *Christmas Beach Proposal.* If you enjoyed the book, we would love it if you gave us a review. Reviews help authors so much. You are appreciated!

Much love,

Lori and Cassidy

ABOUT THE AUTHORS

Cassidy Grace is bursting onto the romance scene with her debut Christmas novella, written with veteran author, Lori Wilde, that proves it's never too late for love.

When this busy mom from Texas isn't driving her kids to soccer practice or volunteering at the local animal shelter, you can find her bringing to life feel-good love stories featuring plucky heroines and handsome strangers.

Cassidy draws inspiration from her own second-chance at romance later in life, proving that passion has no expiration date. An avid reader since childhood, storytelling is in Cassidy's veins, and she can't wait to warm your heart this holiday season with tales of laughter, hope, and Christmas cheer in her small-town Texas setting.

Lori Wilde is the New York Times, USA Today and Publishers' Weekly bestselling author of 97 works of fiction. She's a three time Romance Writers' of

America RITA finalist and has four times been nominated for Romantic Times Readers' Choice Award. She has won numerous other awards as well. Her *Wedding Veil Wishes* series has inspired six movies from Hallmark.

Kael

Truman

Dan

Rex

Clay

Jonah

Made in the USA
Columbia, SC
07 October 2024

43824210R00105